MAKING RAISINS DANCE

Sylvia Weiss Sinclair

Sylvia Weiss Sinclair

Jan-Carol
Publishing, Inc
"every story needs a book"

Making Raisins Dance
Sylvia Weiss Sinclair

Published August 2018
Little Creek Books
Imprint of Jan-Carol Publishing, Inc.
All rights reserved
Copyright © 2018 Sylvia Weiss Sinclair

ISBN: 978-1-945619-65-6
Library of Congress Control Number: 2018950330

You may contact the publisher:
Jan-Carol Publishing, Inc.
PO Box 701
Johnson City, TN 37605
publisher@jancarolpublishing.com
jancarolpublishing.com

To my two sons, David and Kenny, who grew up to be fine men.
And to all the junior high school students in Los Angeles
whom I taught, once upon a time.

Dear Reader

Making Raisins Dance is based on my experiences teaching at an "at-risk" junior high school in Los Angeles, California. The Dancing Raisins experiment was the turning point of my short career teaching Science and Math to students that were Limited English Proficient, known as LEP students, and English as a Second Language, known as ESL students. All events are true to the best of my knowledge and memory. That said, I consider this a work of fiction. I have changed the names of all locations, including the name of the junior high school. In addition, all characters are fictionalized by changing names or composites of students I taught. It is my hope that I made a difference in those young lives by giving them visual examples of Math and Science through classroom experiments, and perhaps sparking their interest to pursue careers in those fields.

Acknowledgments

A big thank you goes out to my publisher, Janie C. Jessee, for seeing the value of my manuscript and having a willingness to publish it. To my brother, Norman, who knows me and my struggles as a first-year teacher so well. Norman, who was a teacher and attended the same junior high school in Los Angeles as I did, that one brief week in 1958. Norman, who with brutal honesty edited my story, thank you, big brother.

Thank you to my old college roommate, Roomie-Zoomie for all the love and support, and all the coffee and pastries that kept me going. Thank you to my mentor teacher, who helped me in so many ways. Thank you, Phil the Physics teacher, who gave me lesson plans in Science. And lastly, I thank my mother, who always believed in me and encouraged me to follow my dreams.

Table of Contents

Prologue

The economic law of supply and demand dictates the lesser the supply of a commodity, the greater the demand. The inverse is also true, the greater the supply, the lesser the demand. This holds true for professions as well, including newly credentialed teachers.

In 1993, the school districts in Orange County had too many teachers and not enough money in their budgets to pay them all. Most school districts laid-off new teachers without seniority and placed a hiring freeze on all positions. Many newly credentialed teachers were forced to look for work in other school districts outside of Orange County, California.

In Los Angeles County, the situation was the opposite. Teachers who were members of the union threatened to strike for more money and benefits. It could get ugly, especially for those non-union teachers who attempted to cross the picket lines. Recent gang riots in the streets of Los Angeles were another reason why teachers in the Los Angeles School District left the teaching profession for safer occupations. Substitutes were called in, but many did not last more than a day or two.

Mrs. Vierma, a science teacher at one of the inner city junior high schools, was one of the teachers who left the profession. Mrs. Vierma never returned to her classes after that fateful day she so frantically screamed out, "*SECURITY! SECURITY!*" But no one came to her aid. The new school term was starting, and Mrs. Vierma's classes already used up four substitute teachers in as many days. Someone had to teach her classes at John Quincy Junior High School, but who?

Maybe someone who could make raisins dance.

1

CHAPTER 1

A TEACHER?

S ofie Richmond, a divorced-poor, woman of forty-six, needed a job. She had invested her meager alimony on graduate classes at the university in Santa Ana to change careers, hoping to find financial security as a secondary school teacher. She suffered through a year of graduate classes and student teaching in the roughest high school in Orange County, only to find there were no jobs in her area. Frustration and disappointment replaced Sofie's optimistic outlook on her future career as a teacher. Months passed since finishing her student teaching. She applied to every school district in Orange County without so much as an interview.

Now, with her savings depleted and student loans to pay off, she needed a real job — a teaching job that paid. Sofie was desperate and ready to go anywhere just to get started. She heard from a friend, Los Angeles School District was hiring.

The next morning, Sofie planned to drive to Los Angeles just to fill in an application for a job teaching, even though it was a long distance from her home.

***

Sofie stares at her tall, thin reflection in the mirror as she steps out of the shower. Her dark coppery-red hair, freshly shampooed, hangs to her shoulders. She wipes the steam from the bathroom mirror and looks closer at her green eyes and her milky white complexion, scattered with freckles

3

wherever the sun kissed her face. She does not look forty-six years old, not with that face and hair. She lost another ten pounds only because she was short on money and she was living on the three Ps: pancakes, potatoes, and popcorn, trying to conserve her cash until she lands a job with a paycheck.

"There just must be a teaching job out there for me," Sofie says to her reflection in the mirror, shaking the little bottle of creamy, beige liquid-makeup. Unscrewing the cap, she places a finger over the opening and shakes it again, then dabs it over her freckles on her nose. Carefully she smooths the foundation over the rest of her face, then grabs the cocoa-brown mascara and combs the bristles through her eye lashes with her mouth wide open. *Now for the lipstick, nothing too gaudy,* Sofie thinks, and picks a peachy color for her lips. Then after washing the makeup off her hands, she reaches for her contact lens case, unscrews the top, and fingers one small contact lens. Carefully, she places it on her left eye. She blinks a few times, getting her focus, and then does the same for her right eye. "There," Sofie says to herself out loud, stepping back to take a better look. She clutches her blow dryer, turns her head upside down and blows the wetness out of her long red tresses. Lifting her head, she straightens her back, then pulls back a few strands in a tortoiseshell hair clip. "Now," Sofie says to her face in the mirror, "what to wear? Let's see; better dress for success."

Glancing at the clock, she sucks in a deep breath, then heads for her closet. She chooses her wool, black and white herringbone suit, black stockings and black pumps with three-inch heels. She starts to dress quickly, pulling on her skirt then stops. "Almost forgot the deodorant," Sofie says. Racing back to the bathroom, she grabs her fresh scent deodorant. She pulls off the cap and swipes each armpit with the waxy stick. Then she reaches for her Sweet Pea body splash and squirts the sweet scent on herself randomly. She likes its fresh springy smell and hopes it will bring her good luck in landing a teaching job. "Gah! I forgot to brush," she says mildly disgusted. Dropping the body spray, Sofie grabs her toothbrush and squeezes some paste on it, then shoves it into her mouth and brushes violently. The mint taste of the toothpaste fills her mouth. She glances at the clock in the bathroom again, spits paste into the sink, rinses, then applies lipstick again. She finishes dressing and steps into her shoes. Finally, she is ready for the long drive to Los Angeles.

Chapter 2

"IT'S A TEACHER!"

The school district office is in the heart of downtown, a large, brick building, built in the 1920's in the middle of skyscrapers. Sofie parks and walks briskly up the great stone steps, her arms clutching a manila folder full of vital papers, credentials, recommendations, and student teaching reviews. She takes a deep breath and summons her confidence, if there is a teaching job, she is going to get it. Through the double glass doors, into the lobby, she glances up at the high ceiling and the rows of opaque windows along the walls, then down to the black and white, hexagon tiled floor. She feels the cold, dampness of the old building, and shivers.

"Can I help you?" asks the woman behind the large, oak desk in the lobby. She puts down her lipstick and compact mirror. Her brown eyes are perfectly outlined under her arched brows, and black shining hair frames her brown face. The bright red of her short sleeve dress, and overpowering smell of perfume, brings Sofie back to reality. She glances at the name plate on the desk which reads, *Yvette Martinez, Receptionist*.

"Why, yes," Sofie says confidently clutching her manila folder. "I'm here to apply for a job, Ms. Martinez."

"Classified or certificated?"

"What's the difference?" Sofie asks, her confidence slipping.

"Classified employment is...well, basically, it's clerical," the receptionist says candidly. "Certificated employment is teaching."

"Certificated, of course," Sofie says, straightening up her back, her confidence returning.

"Go down this hall then turn left. The Human Resources department is the first door on your right," the receptionist directs. Then Ms. Martinez returns to applying the dark red lipstick and gazing at her plump red lips in her compact mirror.

As Sofie walks down the hall, she can hear the *click-click, click-click* of her heels on the tile. Her mind wanders as she thinks how the black and white, hexagon tiled floor, matches her black and white herringbone suit. She turns left, as instructed, then walks to the door on her right. As she reaches for the door, she feels her stomach churning. Turning the knob, she pulls open the door to reveal another large room with a high ceiling. Twenty rows of wooden chairs fill the room, parted in the middle, with only two other people seated. A tall black man in a dark blue suit sits towards the front, and a heavy set Mexican woman in a floral print dress sits in the very last row. In front of all the chairs is a long low counter, and several desks separated by partitions. The room is silent, except for the clicking of Sofie's black high heel shoes as she walks between the rows of chairs. She approaches a small Japanese woman wearing all black, sitting behind the counter.

"I am here to apply for *certificated* employment, as a secondary teacher." Sofie tells the Japanese woman, emphasizing the newly learned word 'certificated,' with a smile.

"Let me see your paperwork," the woman behind the counter says, grimly looking over her red plastic framed glasses at Sofie.

Sofie stops smiling and hands the woman her manila folder.

The woman behind the counter glances through Sofie's folder, then looks up at Sofie and tells her to sit down and wait.

Sofie turns and walks back to one of the chairs in the third row and sits down. She feels a drop of sweat, trickling down her armpit. She takes a deep breath and prays her deodorant will not fail her. In her nervousness, she fingers a strand of her long red hair, twisting it into a curl. *Why didn't I put my hair up in a bun*, she thinks to herself. *It would look more professional.* She pops a breath mint into her mouth for breath insurance, tasting the mint flavor spreading over her tongue and the roof of her mouth.

"Sofie Richmond?"

7

Sofie looks up with a start, and then stands. In front of her is a Hispanic man about four inches shorter than she. *Why did I wear those three-inch heels?* She feels like a giant next to the man facing her, with black spiked hair, a neatly trimmed mustache, and beard. As she looks down at him, she notices his black wire-framed eyeglass sitting on the bridge of his nose, his brown eyes peering over the tops of his glasses. He is wearing a brown tweed suit, a white shirt, and a blue and brown stripped tie. His brown leather shoes are shined to a high gloss.

"Yes, that's me," says Sofie, smelling his Armani cologne and feeling that queasy feeling in the pit of her stomach again.

"I am Mr. Guzman," says the man with the beard and mustache. "Follow me," he commands. To Sofie, Mr. Guzman resembles a short Latino version of Jesus Christ. Was he telling Sofie to be his disciple, and teach the Hispanic children of Los Angeles the lessons of math and science?

Sofie wants to say, she can only teach, not walk on water, but she says nothing. She bites her lip to keep from saying something stupid and follows the small Latino Christ through the electric gate in the long counter separating the teacher candidates from those who had the power to turn them into real, paid teachers. They walk back to a small gray cubicle with one small metal desk and two chairs, one on either side of the desk.

"Sit down," Mr. Guzman, says pointing to a wooden chair in front of his desk and sits down behind his desk in a leather, swivel chair. He opens Sofie's manila folder and starts reading through her files. "It's a teacher!" he mutters to himself out loud, his eyes widening. "And she's taught before!" He seems surprised and delighted, like opening a present on Christmas morning and getting exactly what he always wanted.

Then turning to Sofie, his eyes narrowing, he looks over his black wire-framed eyeglasses and says to Sofie, "Are you sure you want to do this?"

"Sure! That's why I'm here," Sofie answers assertively, and then adds, "I used to live in Los Angeles when I was a kid."

"Oh. Whereabouts?" inquires Mr. Guzman.

"Arapahoe Street, near Hoover and Pico," Sofie replies.

"How would you like to work in your old neighborhood?" Mr. Guzman asks guardedly, his eyes narrowing again, as he strokes his beard and mustache.

"Sure, that would be too cool!" Sofie replies instantly. She has not been in the old neighborhood for many years. The freeway took her parents' house in the 1950s, and her family moved to the suburbs. Her curiosity piqued, she wonders what the old neighborhood looks like now. She has lots of childhood memories of living on Arapahoe Street.

"Welcome back," Mr. Guzman tells Sofie with a grin.

"Thanks," Sofie says as she snaps out of her daydream.

"Just take the elevator up to the second floor and go through the double doors to the right," Mr. Guzman instructs, "and they will give you the name and location of three schools to interview for teaching positions in math or science." Then he adds, "Good luck!" Mr. Guzman stands and reaches out his hand, as if to seal the bargain.

Stunned, Sofie stands and shakes Mr. Guzman's hand, then turns and walks to the electric gate. The small Japanese woman buzzes the gate and Sofie pushes it open. She walks out of the large room in a daze, muttering to herself, "Is that all there is to it? Wow, that was easy."

Out in the hallway, Sofie looks to the right, and sure enough, there is the elevator. Impatiently, she pushes the *up* button several times, then the doors slide open. She enters the elevator and punches the number 2 button and waits for the doors to close. Slowly the elevator creaks up to the second floor and stops with a jerk and a groan. Another wait and finally the doors part. Sofie exits the ancient lift and looks to her right and there are the double doors, where her teaching career will begin. She will get referrals to three schools that need science teachers, right here in Los Angeles. It was that easy. All those classes and lesson plans finally will be used in a paying teaching job. Sofie just can't wait.

***

What Sofie does not know that day, is she will be assigned to John Quincy Junior High School and given Mrs. Vierma's math and science classes. Mrs. Vierma called in sick one day and never returned.

***

9

Sofie's confidence returns to her posture, walking head held high through the double doors to her right, as instructed by Mr. Guzman. A tall, well-dressed, black woman in a navy-blue suit comes up to Sofie. "Are you Sofie Richmond?" the woman asks.

"Why yes," Sofie answers. "That's me."

"Good. Here are the names of three schools in the district who need math and science teachers, and the principals of those schools to contact," the woman replies. "Just call the principals and make appointments to interview for the positions."

Looking down at the list of schools, Sofie is surprised, one junior high now in session and in need of a science teacher immediately, is the same one Sofie attended thirty-five years ago.

"Strange," she says to the woman, "I went to this junior high school, John Quincy, when I was a kid," pointing to one school on her referral list.

The tall, black woman smiles, and says, "Well, welcome back."

CHAPTER 3

THE OLD NEIGHBORHOOD

John Quincy Junior High is the school Sofie plans to interview with first. She feels a wave of nostalgia as she drives to the junior high school she attended for only one brief week in February 1958. Her thoughts begin to wander as she drives north on the Santa Ana freeway in morning traffic, toward her old neighborhood.

***

She remembers her two older brothers attending John Quincy before her, telling tales of fights everyday after school. Sometimes they were chased by gangs on the way home, throwing dirt clods and rocks. Her brothers grabbing cardboard boxes to put over their heads when passing through the war zone. At the time, most students were black or Hispanic and Sofie, being lily white, was terrified. At eleven years old, she was tall and lanky, her thick red hair and glasses made her the perfect target to bully and tease. Most black girls her age had reached puberty and were bigger and stronger than Sofie.

Her battles with the other girls were torturous. Sofie could not forget the day in the fifth grade when, Brenda, one of the bigger black girls, argued with her on the softball field. Sofie was playing second base, and Brenda was up. Brenda hit one low toward third base, she touched first base and was heading for second. Nicole was on third, caught the ball and threw it straight

11

to Sofie on second base. Sofie caught the ball, and just as Brenda was sliding in on second base, Sofie tagged Brenda out. Brenda said she was safe. Sofie said she was out. Words started flying, then pushing and shoving, and then fists were swinging.

The kids on the playground circled the two scrapping girls. The entertainment was on, as the crowd yelled:

"Fight!" "Fight!"

"Get her, Brenda!"

"Look at that white girl fight!"

"That white girl, she sure can fight!"

Then Brenda caught hold of Sofie's long red ponytail and started whipping her around like a wet rag, dragging her to the ground. Hot tears of anger welled up in Sofie's eyes. She couldn't break free.

Just when Sofie thought she could take no more, Mrs. Farley, the playground monitor, saw the crowd of kids and came running. "Alright, now, what's going on here? Break it up. Go on, get going."

Then turning to Sofie and Brenda, her brows knitted, asks, "Now girls, what exactly happened here?" And before either girl could answer, the bell rang, bringing an end to recess. Mrs. Farley gave them both a piercing stare and said, "Go on now, and get to class. Don't let me catch you fighting again, or it's off to the principal's office for the both of you."

And with that, they both stalked off to class. When they were out of earshot of Mrs. Farley, Brenda threatened Sofie, "If you tell your teacher about this, I'll get you after school."

***

Now Sofie's thoughts drift to how much John Quincy Junior High School resembled a prison. The junior high school is so large; it takes up two city blocks, and is completely fenced in. There are buildings two and three stories high. With so many buildings and classrooms, she never saw a single soul from her elementary school. Only one week after she started school at John Quincy Junior High, her parents moved the family to Glenoaks, an all-white suburb of Los Angeles with not a black face in sight.

The traffic on the freeway slows to a stop, then starts up again, only to stop again. There is an accident up ahead. Sofie's thoughts drift again back to her childhood. She and her brothers went to this rough junior high, and all three went on to graduate from college and build careers on that education. *There is always hope*, she rationalizes.

Education is the key to prosperity and harmony. Her father was an immigrant from Eastern Europe, who dropped out of school in the eleventh grade during the depression to help support his family. Her mother, raised in the South on a farm by immigrant parents, only finished the eighth grade. *We were the first on both sides of the family to go to college. Surely if we could make it, I could inspire my students to strive for a better lifestyle through education. After all, college is only a test of endurance. You just must stick it out, through thick and thin, and do all the work, and you can graduate. The key is to want to learn, more than anything else. Motivation.*

"Motion. Will traffic ever move?" she shouts out loud with her windows rolled up. "There. Finally, the tow trucks arrived. Now, traffic is starting to move again." Slowly at first, then around the wreck, and now cars are moving at a fast clip. "Watch the signs now, Sofie," she mutters to herself. "the exit is coming up soon."

As she pulls off the freeway, she sees the homeless people holding up signs that read, *Will Work for Food. Thank You and God Bless.* Both black and white men carry signs, with their hands out. The Mexicans are selling oranges, peanuts, flowers or anything to earn a buck; they never beg.

Approaching the old neighborhood where Sofie lived the first twelve years of her life, she notices changes. What once was a lower middle-class, racially mixed neighborhood being now a Hispanic barrio of the working-poor. All buildings within a radius of thirty blocks of her old neighborhood, display multiple gangland tagging in large bold lettering and colorful graffiti to claim gang territories. Names of gangs and their members proliferated the area, written with anything that leaves a mark on anything that does not move. Moving objects, such as buses and trucks, are also targets for tagging. The technique for tagging in motion is to hop on the back of the moving vehicle, spray paint the gang name or logo, then jump off. No sign is too tall to tag. The only signs immune to gangland tagging are those with barbed wire coiled around their bases. Nothing is sacred, not trees, not churches, nothing. No sooner than a merchant paints over the graffiti, another tagging crew hits the following night.

Soon the school is in sight. Sofie glances down the street to see an old ragged black man pushing a shopping cart full of all his worldly positions. Sofie feels a lump in the pit of her stomach, as she circles the school once. "Do I really want to do this, this teaching thing, here, in the center of the urban jungle?" she questions herself out loud.

Then her eye catches the sight of something she did not know existed. "My God," she says. "There's the tunnel, the tunnel that has haunted my dreams since childhood!" The tunnel connects the main campus to the playground on the next block. Students can safely cross to the other side through the tunnel under the busy street.

After moving from the old neighborhood, Sofie would dream of the tunnel, repeatedly. The dream is always the same. She is a child, walking along, minding her own business. Then she feels someone following her, someone meaning to harm her. Soon she is walking faster, looking back over her shoulder to see several large creepy men following her. The faster she walks the faster her followers walk. She breaks into a run, running as fast as she can, gasping for breath, her followers hot on her trail, not far behind. Nowhere to hide, looking for some way of eluding her pursuers, she sees the tunnel, the dank smell of motor oil and piss in the dark tunnel filling her nostrils. Glancing back, her pursuers are right behind her, chasing her, gaining, getting closer and closer. *The tunnel. Try to lose them through the tunnel,* her instincts tell her. Making a mad dash, running, as fast as she can, she ducks into the tunnel. Once inside the long, dark tunnel, the air feels cold, damp and clammy on her skin. Her energy spent, she slows to a jog, then to a walk. Cautiously, quietly, she walks in the darkness, glancing around, the moist, black walls of the tunnel, dripping with moisture, smelling now like mildew and rotting fish. The putrid smell turns her stomach. She looks to the far end of the tunnel and sees a faint light far in the distance. Walking for some distance, the light grows in diameter, and now she can hear something, some faint noise in the far distance. As she nears the end of the tunnel, the noise seems to sound like music, ever so faintly at first, growing louder as she gets closer to the end.

Emerging on the other side of the tunnel into the open air and sunshine, she finds a carnival going on. She sees a huge merry-go-round, lots of game booths and hears a band playing music. The whole playground on the other side of the tunnel is filled with music and lots of people dancing and singing along. Her followers emerge from the tunnel shortly after her. They look around, but do not see her as she peeks behind the ticket booth.

Then she awakes. The fear of being chased and beaten up after school comes out in her dreams. All the stories her brothers told about gangs in the old neighborhood and being chased materialized in her dreams. And now, here she is, at the scene of her nightmares.

"Do I really want to teach here, at the junior high school I feared so much as a child?" She asks herself again. She takes a deep breath, looks in the mirror, "God, I was only there for a week when I was eleven years old. I'm grown now. Where's the harm? Besides, it is only an interview. It's good practice for when the right job comes along," She rationalizes. "They may not even want me." She hopes. So, she parks the car on the street, walks to the main entrance of John Quincy Junior High School, and bravely walks in.

CHAPTER 4

THE INTERVIEW

Entering through the heavy metal door of John Quincy Junior High School in the heart of the barrio, Sofie is amazed at how clean the school appears. She sees no tagging anywhere, inside the ancient building or on the outside. The school buildings, over one hundred years old, seem freshly painted and well maintained. She runs her index finger along the grey-green walls as her high heel pumps, make a clicking sound on the polished grey floor. Two short Latino ladies in dark blue slacks and white button up blouses walk up to Sofie, greeting her at the front entrance of the school. Their faces are void of make-up except for bright red lipstick on their brown skin. One of the ladies wears her course, blue-black hair in a short cut, while the other lady wears her long, dark brown hair neatly braided and looped on either side. They have a no-nonsense look about them.

"What is your business here," the lady with the short hair asks sharply.

"I have an interview with the principal," Sofie says meekly, clearly intimidated by these guardians of the school.

"Just walk down that hall and the first door to your right, you'll see a sign over the door that says 'Office'. You can't miss it," the lady with the long, braided hair replies kindly, pointing the way.

The office is a busy place, full of teachers signing in, using phones, while students help behind the counter. Sounds of phones ringing, people chattering, copy machines noisily cranking out copies of lesson plans, handouts, and tests fill the air. In the back room, administrators are doing whatever they do, mostly staying out of the way. A student worker comes up to Sofie

16

at the counter and asks, "Can I help you?" She is wearing jeans and a t-shirt with the school logo on the pocket. Her long brown hair is swept up in a ponytail and her hazel eyes sparkle under thick bangs hanging just above her eyebrows.

"I am Sofie Richmond. I have an interview with Mrs. Castillo, the principal," Sofie answers, straightening her posture and throwing back her shoulders.

The student disappears, then returns, handing Sofie a three-page form, and says, "Fill this out and Mrs. Castillo will be with you in a few minutes."

True to her word, Mrs. Castillo appears shortly, ushering Sofie into her small windowless office. Another administrator, Emma O'Brien joins the two ladies, closing the door behind her and locking out all the noise.

Mrs. Castillo is a tall, thin, elegant Hispanic woman in her fifty's, well dressed in a dark olive suit and a cream-colored blouse underneath. Her shoulder length dark brown hair is perfectly coiffed. She is soft spoken when she offers Sofie a seat. The other administrator, Miss O'Brien, is a plain looking Anglo lady in her late thirties, her dirty blonde hair cut short. The tan slacks and pale blue polo shirt on her thin frame, give her a boyish appearance. Miss O'Brien follows Sofie into the room and asks her to take a seat. After everyone is seated, Mrs. Castillo remarks to Emma, "She's credentialed, and she's taught before." Then turning to Sofie, she says, "We have an immediate opening in our math department. What kind of lesson plans do you have for junior high math? And discipline, how do you maintain discipline in your classroom? Also, tell us, why do you want to teach, especially this grade and in the heart of L.A."

Sofie is ready. She takes out her portfolio and knows her best sales pitch down pat. She practiced it so many times in the mirror, she memorized every word. Sofie takes a deep breath, feeling her lungs expand, and launches into her prepared speech. "Well, Mrs. Castillo, I was born and raised in Los Angeles. I attended this very junior high when I was a kid." Sofie did not need to tell Mrs. Castillo she only attended John Quincy for a week. "I went on to college and had a very successful job as well-paid accountant."

She takes another deep breath and continues. "But something was missing in my life. I feel lucky I had great teachers in junior high school, and

I want to give something back to kids that age. I believe junior high school is the turning point on whether students will be successful in high school or drop out. I see these kids as ugly ducklings, blossoming into swanhood. It is here, in junior high school, kids begin to form their identity, and our job as educators is to give them a vision of their future. Education is like a dance, sometimes two steps forward, and one step backward. An effective teacher must be flexible to reach all students, not just the ones who want to learn, but all students, not allowing any to fall through the cracks. Education, it's a dance."

By the smiles on their faces and nods of agreement, Sofie feels she is holding her small but powerful audience of two in the palm of her hand. She is in rare form.

Looking down at Sofie's resume, Miss O'Brien's blue-green eyes widens. She sees Sofie majored in chemistry with three years of chemistry and other science classes under her belt. Turning to Mrs. Castillo excitedly, then to Sofie, she says, "How about the math/science position opening in the other track?"

"Sure," Sofie says confidently. "That would be really fun and very exciting. If I teach both math and science, maybe we can do something like this?" That's when Sofie whips out her portfolio and opens it to the 8 X 10 glossy photo of the NASA rocket launching along with photos of Sofie and her students on the field trip to Vandenberg Air Force Base. There is even a personal note from NASA's public relations person.

That is when Mrs. Castillo offers Sofie the job and tells Miss O'Brien, "Lock the door, Emma!" Then looking Sofie straight in the eyes, she says, "And Ms. Richmond, don't you dare interview with any other schools."

Sofie is stunned. Composing herself, she says, "Wow. Well, let me think about this. I will give you a call back in the next couple of days and give you my decision." Sofie sits there before the two administrators, her mind spinning. *School starts in two weeks*, she thinks to herself, *if I take this job, there is still lots of paperwork to fill out at the school district. Should I throw caution to the wind and accept this offer, a real paid teaching contract? Am I crazy enough to drive one hundred and twenty miles a day to teach junior high school students in the trenches of Los Angeles, where nobody, especially from Orange County, dare to teach? Somebody must teach these kids*, she tells herself, *if there is ever going to be hope for the future.* And so, for an instant, temporary insanity overtakes reason and Sofie blurts out, "Yes, I'll teach here!"

CHAPTER 5

DOCUMENTED AND FINGERPRINTED

Sofie drives three more trips to downtown to the school district's office before she is officially ready to teach. She sits waiting, while the clock ticked away the hours. Dealing with the Los Angeles School District is like trying to move a giant slug, extremely slow and slippery. After the interview, all the paperwork must be completed and turned in before she can start teaching. She is required submit her secondary teaching credential, proof of citizenship, as well as her immunization records. Sofie finishes filling in all the little tiny boxes on every conceivable form, then she is fingerprinted like a common criminal, and required to take the oath of allegiance. By that time, school has started.

Sofie knows she wants to teach more than anything else in the world. To her, teaching is the only profession you can change young lives and make a difference and get the bonus of having summers off!

However, what Sofie does not know is, the first four days of the new semester, her assigned classes have been taught by four different substitute teachers. Each one leaving at the end of each day, vowing never to teach those kids again.

Assigned to Mrs. Vierma's classes, Sofie is hired under an emergency credential for physical science and math, so she is to teach under a provisional contract. None the less, it is a teaching contract and she is thrilled. A provisional contract grants Sofie all the benefits of a real teacher, insurance, sick leave and the coveted reward, the summers off.

Oh, how she savors the idea of teaching five hours a day, and then traveling during the summer, while the whole world works. The summers off has the feel of the warm sunshine, basking in the sun after a dip in the cool ocean waves, the smell of tropical tan oil, caressing her tan, bare skin. But every paradise has its serpent. Sofie's serpent is six more units in the physical sciences to complete, to renew her yearly teaching contract.

But, for now, Sofie is finally all set to teach her first paid classes. She is so excited she hardly sleeps the night before, scratching out lesson plans in her loose-leaf notebook for each class. Practicing in front of the bathroom mirror what to say and how to say it. Watching her reflection carefully, her hair, does it look okay? She can feel a knot tightening in her stomach.

It is the night before her first class. She thinks, *a hot bath and a good sleep will smooth out all my tension and anxiety. Humm, what to wear on my first day? I'd better get that all sorted out tonight.* Sofie leaves the bathroom and heads for her walk-in closet. *A suit will do nicely.* Fingering through her wardrobe, she studies the colors of her skirts and jackets she wore when working in an office. "Red, teal, brown tweed, blue," she mutters to herself. "Blue, that's it. Trust me blue. True blue. That's what I will wear on the first, most important day of my new career, my blue suit. Now for shoes," she says, talking to herself, again. "Black high heeled shoes. The right shoes for that dress-for-success look. Black corporate, accountant shoes will do perfectly," feeling the smooth black leather, as she runs her hand over her favorite shoes.

Then Sofie hunts through her closet, under the piles of shoes, and purses, until she finds her black leather briefcase. She grabs one of her pink terry cloth towels out of the bathroom and wipes the dust and dirt off. Opening it, she smells the musky odor of mildewing leather, "Uck! Smells like I'll need some Lysol here to wipe out the mildew." Cautiously, Sofie wipes the inside of her briefcase and dries it with another rag. Then she carefully places her precious teacher's edition of the physical science and math textbooks inside the briefcase. Next, she puts in her notebook with lesson plans and a hand full of pens and pencils. She is ready, or so she thinks.

She runs a bath and drops some lavender oil into the water; the sweet smell of flowers fills the little blue and white tiled bathroom. She pulls off her sweats and steps into the tub, letting her naked body relax in the warm, fragrant water. Her thoughts drift now, thinking of cozy, flannel pajamas, soft fluffy pillows, and warm fuzzy bedding. She hopes sleep will come soon when she crawls into bed that night.

CHAPTER 6

DRESSED FOR SUCCESS

Friday morning, Sofie reports to the attendance office of John Quincy Junior High School one half hour before classes start. She stands at the wooden counter in her nice, true-blue suit and her black, high heel, dress-for-success, corporate accountant shoes. With the help of a luggage carrier, she totes a bag full of textbooks and her briefcase strapped to the top with a red and white bungee cord.

"Hi. I'm Sofie Richmond, the new teacher for physical science and math," she says to the student aide behind the counter. She is feeling ready and confident for her first day of teaching.

"Oh, Ms. Richmond, so *you're* the one taking of over Mrs. Vierma's classes," the student aide says with surprise. She smirks a little behind her red lipstick, her dark eyes laughing. "Here's your schedule and room assignment, Ms. Richmond. Oh, here's a map of the school campus. Your room is right here," pointing to room 327. "It's on the third floor of this here building at the far end of the campus. Good luck."

"Thanks," says Sofie, staring down at the map. Sofie looks up at the girl with a weak smile and the girl smiles back a bit too cheerily. Sofie stares back at the map and realizes it is a long distance to her room from the office.

Well, I see I will have to trudge three flights of stairs up and one flight down to get to my classroom. Sofie thinks about walking up and down flights of stairs in her favorite high heel shoes, not to mention the twenty pounds of books strapped her little cart and her impressive black briefcase bungy corded to the top of the stack.

The reward for that morning's "stair-step" exercise is a small, grey classroom with windows overlooking the street below. Once breathlessly up in her own room with only five minutes to the bell, Sofie glances at her schedule of classes, nervously shuffling through all the papers she has pulled out of in her mailbox in the office on her first day.

"Seventh grade math is first, then homeroom," she mutters to herself while there is no one around. "Conference period is next, then nutrition. Third period is eighth-grade science, fourth period, ninth-grade science, then comes lunch. Algebra is fifth period and then another eighth-grade science class. That makes four preps, four different subjects to prepare for, four different lesson plans. Ache. This is going to be a lot of work," she moans.

Rrriiinnnggg

"Oh! It's the bell!" She cries out loud, panic starting to set in. Sofie feels that knot in her stomach, aching from nervousness.

They're coming in! A little voice inside her head squeaks, as she hears the students trample through the door like a herd of buffalo.

What do I do? Sofie's mind is spinning, trying to remember all the things she learned in the credentialing classes. *Quick, my name on the board! That's right. Just like I practiced for the past two nights. And something else, what is it? Oh, yes, some sort of assignment. Write something on the board to keep them busy while I take roll. That's it. Hey, I'm a teacher!*

Gaining her composure, Sofie walks up to the black board, picks up the yellow chuck of chalk and begins to print her name in bold block letters, **MS. RICHMOND.** Then as she starts to copy math problems on the board, the chalk breaks from the force of the pressure Sofie uses. It shatters into pieces and falls to the floor. Sofie feels her face flush, when she hears laughter from the back row. She grabs another piece of chalk and starts to write on the board again, this time with a little less pressure. She uses a list of math problems out of the book involving adding, subtracting, multiplication, and division. She hopes the problems will keep the students busy long enough to take roll.

As the students pour into the small classroom with five rows of desks, Sofie eyes the students, eyeing her back; both wondering what is to come. The room is alive with seventh grade junior high school students, bursting with energy and chatter, bouncing off the walls. Some making "kick me" signs to put on unsuspecting classmates for a joke. Others manufacturing paper airplanes to launch at the target, Ms. Richmond, the moment she turns her back to them. Still others talking in English as well as Spanish about events in their young lives past, present, and what is to come. And still others are writing notes to pass on to classmates sitting too far away to talk to without yelling across the classroom. The room is abuzz.

Again, Sofie tries to write problems on the board, when again crash. The yellow chalk shatters. Chalk pieces fall. Sofie makes a mental note to use less pressure when writing with chalk. Another burst of nervous laughter and then silence, as Sofie turns and glares at the class. She picks up another piece of chalk, red in the face now, and finishes writing the problems.

Sofie smiles to herself. *Juniors, of course it is funny to them to see a teacher make a mistake.*

"I am Ms. Richmond..." Sofie begins introducing herself when she is quickly interrupted.

"Are you a sub?" asks several students at once.

For the first four days of school, Mrs. Vierma's students were taught by four different substitute teachers, none willing to come back the following day. Students regard substitute teachers as fresh meat. The students collaborate to see how much they can get away with. They know that subs are here today and gone tomorrow. The students are given worksheets simply to keep them busy.

"No!" Sofie says explicitly. "I am your real teacher for the rest of the semester." With a great deal of pride, Sofie goes on to tell the students she once sat in one of their seats thirty-five years ago, and that she was born and raised in Los Angeles. She continues to talk about herself until she notices the students getting bored and restless. *What do they care about where I came from or who I think I am? That's ancient history, not math. Better get those juniors busy on something, like worksheets.*

25

"Now that you know a little about me..." Sofie says changing the subject. She reaches down and brings out a stack of index cards out from her pile of stuff. Then walking up and down the aisles, she personally hands out a card to each student.

"Now, it is your turn to tell me a little about you. On the card I have given you, print your name, address, phone num..."

"Are you going to call my house and come for dinner?" yells out one student, from the back row where all the bad boys sit. The whole class bursts into laughter.

"No," Sofie shouts back, feeling her face burning with anger. Then softly as an afterthought, "But I may have to call your parents or write them a note on your behavior in class." The class then turns silent, and all the students shuffle around until they are all sitting up straight.

Returning to her instructions, Sofie says, "Now, where were we? Name, first line, address, second line, phone number, third line. On the fourth line, print your parents' names, and if they speak English. If they do not speak English, write down the language they speak? On the next line, write what is the best thing about you, and on the last line, write what was the best thing about the best teacher you ever had. Any questions?" *That should keep them busy for a while.*

"What if you never had any good teachers?" another girl shouts wearing bib overalls and a black long sleeve stretch top underneath. Another burst of laughter from the class.

Through clenched teeth, Sofie answers, "Then tell me, *if* you had a great teacher, what would make that teacher great."

This does not sound good. What have I gotten myself into? A little voice inside Sofie's head speaks to her.

For a few minutes, silence overtakes the classroom. Sofie begins to take roll, stumbling over a few names, and all seems to be going well...at last.

Sofie starts to ask the students to introduce themselves, when another unsolicited comment comes from one of the girls in the front row. "We already know everyone."

"Very well." Sofie sighs, realizing this little introduction game is not working. "Pass the cards forward and start working the problems on the board. What you do not finish is homework." Sofie says, glancing at the clock. She realizes there is twenty-three minutes left of the class. She feels a knot tightening in the pit of her stomach, and tiny drops of perspiration forming in her armpits.

***

Sofie thought all the classes at the university would prepare her for this day, but she was wrong. Nothing prepared her for Mrs. Vierma's classes. Nothing. The kids in Mrs. Vierma's classes were tough and street-wise. Some were already in gangs, others wanted to be. They were already hardened to the world from seeing their friends killed by drive by shootings. Some carried weapons outside the school for protection. Others carried marking pens, to mark off their gang's territories with gang names written on buildings and walls. Many were poor and would steal anything given a chance. But they were *all* good at taunting and tormenting. At least that is what Mrs. Vierma discovered, before she disappeared.

***

Then a thought comes to Sofie about how she can engage her students in a math problem. She goes to the chalk board, careful not to turn her back on the students, the cardinal rule of teaching, and writes the number *35*. Then says to the class, "If I attended this school thirty-five years ago, who can tell me how old I am, and how you figure it out."

Let's see if these kids know how to add and subtract, Sofie says to herself.

"Forty-five!"

"Fifty-five!"

"Sixty-five!"

"A hundred and five!!"

The students are all yelling out numbers at once. Total chaos. Laughing. Talking. Joking. *No control. Not good,* Sofie's thoughts flood her mind. *They are not thinking, they are only blurting numbers out. Not good. Not good at all.*

27

Patiently, Sofie smiles at the pandemonium she has created in the room. Walking up to the green chalk board, she writes the analysis of the problem. Careful not to turn her back on the students, she discusses how to arrive at the right answer.

"What about books?" A short stocky brown skinned boy yells out, raising his hand. Sofie notices he has the look of a street gang: baggy blue jeans slit at the frayed hem and a plaid blue and black flannel long sleeve shirt. His black hair is buzzed short on the sides and grown very long on top, combed straight back.

"What about books? Don't you have your books?" Sofie asks puzzled. *No one at the office told me the kids didn't have books.*

"The teacher collected our math books at the end of last semester," a small thin black boy in jeans and tee shirt answers without raising his hand.

With only a few minutes to the end of the period, Sofie says, "Okay, I'll check on your math books and see if we can get them tomorrow...so I can assign homework."

Rrriiinnnggg, blares the dismissal bell.

"Class dismissed," Sofie shouts, as all but a few students thunder out of the classroom.

"Why are you kids still sitting there," Sofie asks the students remaining after the bell. "Don't you have to get to your next class, Juan?" Sofie is beginning to learn the names of her students, well, at least the first names.

"We *are* in our next class. We have you for our homeroom teacher," answers Juan, a short, pudgy boy with dark curly hair.

"Oh," replies Sofie. "What do you usually do in homeroom?"

"Nothing," answers Maria, as she pulls out a mirror and lip-gloss, then applies the gloss and smacks her lips together.

"Oh," Sofie replies again. And that is exactly what they did. Nothing. Sofie was not told what was to be done in homeroom. The knot in her stomach tightens again as she glances at the names on the roll sheet.

Rrriiinnnggg, the bell sounds again, signifying that everyone should be in their homeroom.

A new set of students thunder in again, all talking at once. Homeroom is only twenty-three minutes long. *Twenty-three minutes until nutrition, Sofie* thinks to herself, *then my conference period, a whole fifty-two minutes. Let's see, she* calculates, *fifty-two minutes and twenty-three minutes, that's seventy-five minutes without students, a whole hour and fifteen minutes. Just twenty-three minutes, I've got to make it through twenty-three minutes of nothing. Can I make it through home-room? God, I hope so.*

"Let's have some silence here, so I can read the bulletin," Sofie shouts over the roar of talking students, while digging through her mass of papers, looking for the daily bulletin. Finally, she finds it, clears her throat and begins reading the bulletin, but no one is listening. Everyone is talking.

"Hey," shouts the tall, skinny boy in the front row, "are you a sub?"

"No. I am your real teacher. Now, let's have it quiet," Sofie shouts back. As she starts reading the bulletin again, the intercom comes on.

"Good morning students," says the cheery voice out of the box above the door. "Today is February twenty-second..." The voice continues reading the bulletin in English and then in Spanish, while all the students continue talking amongst themselves. The noise is deafening.

After the announcements over the intercom ends, Sofie attempts to take roll amid all the noise and confusion. In the front sits a small Hispanic boy, not saying a word, his nervousness is visually obvious. He does not speak a word of English. Sofie learns later he just arrived from El Salvador.

Rrriiinnnggg. Homeroom was over. With the rumbling of chairs and thirty-five pairs of feet, suddenly the room is silent. Sofie looks around her room at the debris of papers, food, candy wrappers, and gum on the floor, left by the first two classes. She breathes a sigh of relief.

"Four more classes to go," she says under her breath. "Ache."

"Ms. Richmond?"

Sofie turns to the voice in the doorway. There stands a tall, older black man, with a very bald head, and wire framed bifocals that made his eyes appear larger than they really are. He is wearing light brown Dockers and a cream-colored polo shirt. His shoes are comfy penny loafers.

"I'm Mr. Randell," he says in a soft voice that does not match his stature or appearance. He is one of the long-term substitutes, hired to fill in the shortage of teachers. "We are supposed to switch classrooms and one class to simplify your schedule."

One of the assistant principals apparently has compassion for Sofie, with her four preps and teaching in a small room on the third floor. They do not want to lose another credentialed teacher.

"Miss O'Brien rearranged your schedule and assigned you to a new classroom. You are moving to the first-floor science building across campus and trading your ninth-grade science class with me in exchange for my third-period eighth-grade physical science class. Now you will only have three preps, and you won't have to climb all those stairs." Mr. Randell adds. "I'm in room eleven and I am taking your ninth-grade science and giving you my eighth-grade science tomorrow."

"How shall we do this?" Sofie asks.

"How about today, we tell all the students to report to the appropriate room today, which is Friday, then Monday we will be ready to teach."

"You mean all of my classes, except my ninth-grade science class, will report to room eleven, and your eighth-grade science class will remain in your room and vice versa?" Sofie clarifies.

"Yes, that's it," Mr. Randell confirms. "I think it will work just fine."

The rest of the day goes by in a state of utter confusion, with the added instruction of the changes in teachers and rooms. Sofie's ninth-grade science is the worst behaved of all her classes that day. Two of the biggest black boys start to duke it out, over something one said to the other. Mr. Randell enters Sofie's room again, just in time to break up the fight. He comes to inform Sofie of yet another change.

"Oh, by the way, Ms. Richmond, we must accompany the classes each period when we move according to the principal. So, all the students should report to their original classrooms. I will walk my students to your classroom and we will exchange classes accordingly."

"That sounds good," Sofie replies. However, there is one slight problem, she already told her third-period class to report to room eleven. To add to the confusion, she told her fourth-period ninth-graders, to stay in the third-floor classroom and exchange teachers. Fifth and sixth period, Sofie decided not to tell them anything.

And so Sofie Richmond's first day at school finally ends. Now her long, long drive home begins. Two hours later, Sofie crawls out of her car with all her books in tow, staggers through the door, heads for the bedroom, and collapses on her bed.

Do I have enough energy to get a bite to eat from the kitchen? she wonders. No. Sleep overtakes her fully clothed, the moment her head hits the pillow. Dreams drift in and out of her head of lesson plans, students, and the move planned for the next school day.

CHAPTER 7

LOST AND CONFUSED

At 4:30 Monday morning, while still dark outside, Sofie's clock radio alarm goes off and hard rock music blares out of its little speaker. *It's time to get up and start getting ready for school?!* Every muscle in her body aches. She drags herself out of bed and stumbles to the bathroom. Turning on the steaming hot water, Sofie strips off the clothes she slept in, then steps into the shower. She stands there for fifteen minutes or so, while her pores soak up the warmth of the water as music drifts into the bathroom through the closed door.

Now clean and awake, she grabs a fluffy yellow bath towel, dries her body, then wraps her purple terry robe around herself. Heading for the kitchen for some morning nourishment, her thoughts turn to vitamins and coffee, *lots of black coffee, oh and maybe toast. Toast is always good. It soaks up the coffee and the vitamins stick to the toast. It all works better that way. Better pack a lunch, and a large thermos full of strong, black coffee, to last through the day. Let's see, better add cream and sugar to sweeten the day.*

Now, the number one question of the morning, what to wear? Sofie ponders. She throws on a dress and a jacket. *Look professional.* Glancing over her shoe wardrobe, she thinks, *Gad, I wish I had some low heel shoes to wear while standing in front of all those kids all day long. Low heel shoes will be the first thing I buy with my first paycheck.* She writes *shoes* on her to-do list and sticks it on her refrigerator with the little magnet shaped like a golden crown with the words

It's good to be Queen printed on it. Yes, *low heel shoes will be very comfy, though probably not very cute,* she thinks.

Into her little, old, red Toyota, Sofie loads her twenty pounds of books strapped to her luggage carrier. As she adjusts her rear-view mirror, she glances at the teacher she is becoming and smiles, then starts her two-hour drive to Los Angeles. She feels ready to make a difference amongst the juniors at John Quincy Junior High. Pride of being a teacher of children, wells up inside her chest. The sun is dawning, and she hears sounds of the commuter traffic, moving slowly through the construction zone, on-going for years. Sofie's ponders, *it is just me and the five million other people in cars, commuting from everywhere to downtown Los Angeles.* The feeling of euphoria about being a new teacher is starting to wear off.

It is still winter in California, and the sun is just coming up in the cold, crisp morning. As Sofie approaches the city, she is awed by the sight in the distance. The sun reflecting off the glass and steel architectural wonders, rising out of downtown like a vision some great artist painted across the sky.

At long, *long* last, Sofie pulls into the parking lot right next to the school entrance. At 7:20AM, there are only two spaces left. Luckily, her car is small and easy to maneuver into one of the remaining slots.

"Let's see," Sofie mutters to herself on the way to the office. "Sign in, check my mail box....What else? Can I get some worksheets photocopied before class? Nope, there's a line already forming at the copy machine. I'll never finish before the bell. Better get to class. Today is the big move."

And so begins Sofie Richmond's second day teaching, up three flights of stairs, down the hall, then down one flight of stairs, with twenty pounds of books and briefcase strapped precariously to her little cart with bungee cords, in high heel shoes.

***

What Sofie Richmond does not know is that moving plans have changed. She is supposed to move into room eight, the former Mrs. Vierma's room, not into room eleven as Mr. Randell has told her. Her third-period class will be meeting in the wrong room. While Sofie stays in her assigned room, taking roll, she waits for Mr. Randell to escort his students to her room. Then, Sofie escorts her students to her new room, room eight, not eleven. Just one more complication to the already complicated plan.

***

When Sofie finally reaches the third floor, nothing looks familiar. *Now, where is my room?* Puzzling over the unfamiliar surroundings. *I'm on the third floor, aren't I? I am supposed to be in room 327 and the numbers only go to 314. Where is my room? I'm lost! I cannot believe this. I feel just like I did thirty-five years ago, starting the seventh grade in a strange, huge school: nervous, lost, and panicked. On no! The bell is ringing! I am going to be late to my own class! I can't find my own class! I can't believe this is happening to me!*

Eying a passing student, Sofie calls out, "Uh, excuse me. Where's room 327?" just as the eight o'clock bell rings. She feels sort of foolish, a teacher asking a student where her room is. But Sofie is desperate. She just does not care how foolish she appears now. She just wants to find her classroom and students.

"I'm going that way," says the cheerful Mexican girl with a wide smile. She's happy to help. "Follow me." Sofie's guide in this strange, new place leads her to the new classroom, where all her students are waiting outside the door.

"You're late," says a boy in baggy jeans, his pants hanging below his waist exposing plaid boxer shorts. He gives his pants a tug to pull them up a bit.

"I know," Sofie replies, embarrassed, as she fumbles with her keys to open the door. Already she is tired, and the day has just begun.

The students pour into the classroom and settle into their chairs with desks attached. The sound of chairs scraping the floor, books dropping on desks and kids chattering in Spanish and English is thunderous.

Sofie tries to get organized quickly. Realizing her class will be moving to another classroom, there is no need to make a seating chart. She starts to call out roll and Mr. Randell appears at the door with all thirty-six of his students. Now the chaos really begins.

Sofie's mind is racing. Tiny drops of sweat are forming on her brow. She feels the flush of panic seizing her. *Quick*, she thinks, *finish* roll, *gather up my twenty pounds of stuff, get the students in two lines, and march them out the door.*

"All right you guys, now listen up," Sofie announces above all the noise. "We're moving to another classroom. Let's form two rows at the door and no talking. I'm taking roll and I need you to say 'here' when your name is called."

"I thought you said no talking?" protests one of the bad boys in the back of the room.

"No talking *except* when you hear your name called. Understand?" says Sofie annoyed at the backtalk.

So, the two rows of students follow their teacher, Ms. Richmond, out the door, down the hall, up one flight of stairs, down three more flights of stairs. The students are all chattering, some rushing ahead to their new destiny, others straggling behind. Sofie's feet already aching in her dress-for-success, black, high heel shoes. Shoes like a vice, squeezing the toes of her poor, unsuspecting feet. These shoes—formerly her favorite—intended to be on the feet of a woman sitting behind at desk all day, staring at a computer screen, occasionally getting up for coffee. Certainly not the feet of a school-marm, to be stood on all day, in a classroom full of juniors, and climbing the mountains of stairs in an ancient school in the heart of Los Angeles.

"Here we are," Sofie tells her troops of students, trying to sound cheerful. "Room eight, our new room." Sofie's thoughts overwhelm her as she thinks, *Gad, how dismal. A room twice as big as the one I left, but twice as ugly. Nothing on the bland, beige walls, except for a few faded health posters, reminding the viewers to brush their teeth, and not to smoke. Who do they think they were fooling? These are junior high school students.*

As Sofie looks around, she also sees two huge avocado green chalkboards, covering almost two complete walls. A third wall embraces a stained sink and counter, with locked cabinets below. To the left are four ceiling to floor cupboards, whose locked double doors are well carved up and marked up with pens by the prior occupants. The four small bulletin boards above the sink and on either side of the green, chalkboards, are covered with faded grayish blue paper. In front of the sink and counter, is a long, heavy, art table, with storage underneath, and all locked. The tabletop itself is heavy and thick, carved, painted, and marked up with names and logos of taggers, covering the grain of the wood. On either side of the "art" table, are two teacher's desks, also carved and tagged, but not to the extent of the other objects in the room.

The room is full of chairs and desk-chairs in various states of disrepair, are also carved and tagged. On the other side of the room is a round table missing one of its three legs, propped against the wall, so as not to tip over. On the back wall are two doors, painted bright orange, letting the occupants in and locking the others out.

A row of small, high windows between the doors let in the daylight, but the last one holds a piece of Plexiglas in its pane, instead of glass. The dirty gray Venetian blinds that cover the small windows are old and battered. The windows on the opposite wall, high above the green, chalkboard, are painted the same bland, beige color of the walls. Several of the painted glass panes have been replaced with wallboard also painted the same bland beige color. The floor is so dirty, it is impossible to tell if there is a pattern to it or not.

Is this the prison cell Sofie is condemned to for being insanely obsessed to teach? Sofie's thoughts swirl around in her brain. Well, at least, it is on the first floor, and students will not try to open windows to climb out, like yesterday, in the third-floor classroom. And, thank goodness, there are no cockroaches that she can see, like the classrooms across the street, in the boys' gym. Mr. Boswell, the teacher she is replacing for math, he had a roach collection of some two hundred specimens, all collected in his classroom.

Think positive, Sofie tells herself. *Someone must teach these children. It might as well be me. Besides, now I am getting paid to teach in this hellhole, not like the student teaching in Santa Ana."*

The class settles in. Sofie gives her seventh grade math students a pretest to work on to see if they can add and subtract without a calculator. The bell rings and the students pour out of the room, leaving papers on and around their desks. A few students still linger, because Sofie has those kids for homeroom. She can't leave students in the room by themselves, but she must go back up to her old third-floor classroom to escort her homeroom to their new classroom. She has seven minutes to find the room before her students.

"Quick, everyone out of the room," she shouts as she shoos the remaining students out.

"Why?" One boy protests. "We have you for next period," he says, as he wipes his runny nose on his sleeve.

"I have to go back up to room three twenty-seven to bring the homeroom down here. Want to come with me?" Sofie asks, hoping at least one student will lead the way.

"Sure," says the boy, all smiles.

"Great! Let's go." Sofie says. She is in luck and relieved that she has a guide.

For the second time that day, Sofie dashes across the campus to the far building, up three flights, down the hall, down another flight of stairs in her high heels. All the time, thinking how she *really* needs to get some low heel shoes, and how her big toe in her left shoe is starting to throb, while the other big toe is completely numb. They barely beat out the bell, but already her audience is starting to form at the door.

Sofie tries to explain the move to her homeroom students, while taking roll. Now Mr. Randell arrives. Sofie starts to line up her students. *Hey, I'm starting to get the hang of this,* she reflects. Now out the door, down the hall, up one flight, down another hall, down three more flights of stairs. *Oh, my aching feet,* are her thoughts while trying to hide the pain. Out onto the quad, across campus to glorious room eight. She fumbles with the keys, and then unlocks the door.

"Yuck," says Marcie, one of the students looking around and smelling the foul air in the classroom. "Is this where we are going to be?" She pulls out a small bottle of spray cologne and sprays the air.

"Yes," Sofie says triumphantly. "This is it!"

"I liked the other room better," retorts Roberto. Roberto is one of the better students, and always meticulously dressed.

The class settles in, and Sofie reads the bulletin, and then gives them "free" time, meaning time to do nothing. Everyone is happy now, chatting with each other about the adventures of the day.

Finally, the bell rings, this time bringing a reprieve of seventy-five minutes without students. Within thirty seconds, the room is empty and quiet again.

37

Sofie gazes at the room that surrounds her and shutters. "Four more classes to go," she whispers under her breath. She shutters thinking, *what have I got myself into this time?*

Time flies by at jet speed as Sofie begins to investigate her new room, opening locked cabinets and cupboards and drawers. Lots of stuff left behind, but nothing she can use. Dazed and confused, Sofie stops and surveys the situation.

"Supplies," she says out loud. "I need pencils, pens, stapler, paper clips. What else? Where do I go to get all the classroom stuff? Oh yes, Chapter One office, in the bungalow across from me. Books, where do I get the books? Books can wait until Monday. Where is that thermos of coffee I brought?" Sofie takes time to unscrew the top of the thermos, and pour out the rich, sweetened, golden brown liquid into an old coffee cup left behind. Coffee always seems to make everything a little better. Slowly, she savors the magic liquid, and begins to feel better already.

The bell rings, and second period is over. "Twenty minutes for nutrition, and then back up the three flights of stairs and down one," she says, going over the route in her mind. She tries to memorize where the classrooms are located. "That's it, up three flights of stairs on the west side, and down one flight of stairs, then back to room 327 again. But wait, didn't I tell my third period science class to meet at room eleven?" Now confusion sets in. "But I am supposed to go to room three...?"

Mr. Randell knocks on the classroom door, and then walks in. "Are you okay Ms. Richmond? You look puzzled."

"Well, I am a little confused about the next move," Sofie admits.

"Just go to room 327 and if the students go to the wrong room, someone will tell them to go to their original room," Mr. Randell advises.

So back she goes. Across campus, into the main building, three flights up, down the hall. *Now, where is the flight down,* she murmurs to herself. *Why does this not look familiar. This is not the right staircase. I can't find my way back to room 327 this way. Better go back the way I started and try again.* So back down the three flights of stairs Sofie races, and down the hall again.

Now this staircase looks more familiar, Sofie mutters with a groan. "Oh, my aching feet." Up another three flights of stairs, down the hall, "*Oh, there it is, the short flight down. Now, how many stairs have I climbed in these crippling high heel shoes? There it is, the room!* Gleefully, she finds her classroom at last.

But the bell is ringing and none of her students are in sight. *Oh no, I guess they all went to room eleven, just like I told them. And here comes Mr. Randell with his students. What's this? Here comes a herd of my students with another adult.*

"Where were you?" the students are all whining and angry for the confusion. "You told us the wrong room."

"What's going on here?" asks the other adult who led Sofie's students. The other adult happens to be Mrs. Bruno, the assistant principal. This does not look good for Ms. Sofie Richmond.

Sofie tries to explain the confusion of the room changes and apologizes to Mrs. Bruno profusely. Sofie feels the blood rush up to her head and change the color of her face from freckled tan to bright crimson.

Mrs. Bruno just rolls her eyes heavenward, then shakes her head in disbelief, leaving the room full of students in Sofie's care.

Sofie clears her throat, adjusts her black plastic framed glasses with a touch of her hand, then tells her class, "We have to go back to Room eight."

"Room eight?!" whines Gregory, the plumpest black boy in the class. "Not again. I'll never make it up and down all those stairs again. I'm *tired.*"

"Maybe you will lose some of that lard around your middle," chides Ricky, a short little Hispanic boy from Mexico. The whole class laughs, and Gregory flushes under his dark skin, obviously embarrassed.

"Hey! Quiet down," Sofie yells back over students' laughter. "I'm tired too. Let's get going, and there will be positively *no* talking in the halls on the way. Understand? Two lines, please. Hurry. We've wasted enough time already."

And so, at last Ms. Sofie Richmond's class is on its way again. Down the hall the troops go in two wobbly lines, up one flight, down another hall, down three more flights of stairs, and so on.

Fourth-period science is even more confusing. Mr. Randell and Ms. Richmond are to switch classes and classrooms, but the students are to remain in their same classroom. They are again to meet their students in the original rooms, take roll, and then move and switch roll books. But how could this be done? Mr. Randell would bring his eighth graders up and Sofie will walk down with them. She is totally confused now.

Sofie begins taking roll, but her ninth-graders are getting restless. Another fight breaks out between the same two big black students. As before, Mr. Randell arrives just in the nick of time, but without the eighth-graders. They are back in Room eight, where Sofie should have gone.

Leaving Mr. Randell to sort out the fight, Sofie dashes down the hall, up one flight, down another hall, down three flights of stairs, out and across campus. She gets to room eight, expecting all students waiting outside, frustrated and angry. Much to her surprise, they are all seated quietly in their seats in room eight. In the back of the classroom stands a giant black man, hovering over the students.

"Am I in the wrong room?" Sofie meekly asks the black man.

He turns to her and demands sternly, "Are you their teacher? What's going on here?"

CHAPTER 8

TEARS FOR FEARS

Holding back the tears, Sofie explains in a fearful voice the circumstances of the past day and a half: She is a new teacher and her classes and classrooms have been changed. She has been up and down a hundred flights of stairs moving students from her old classroom on the third-floor of the main building to here. As she talks to the unknown black man in the back of the room, several students turn to look at her, trying to pick up on their conversation.

"What are you looking at?" booms the giant black man's voice like the ball out of a canon. "Turn around and get back to work!" he fires again. He has given the students worksheets on the body to keep them busy. They turn around in an instant, and the room falls dead silent, as they go back to their worksheets. He turns to Sofie and says in the voice of a comforting father, "I understand. I understand. I'm Mr. Jones, your mentor teacher. The principal, Mrs. Castillo, sent me to look after you, help you out in whatever you need."

"My God!" Sofie's thoughts turn heavenward. *My payers have been answered! A guardian angel. They sent me a guardian angel. Just when I didn't think I could make it through the rest of this day. I have been sent a savior to help me to endure the hardships that come from teaching at-risk kids.*

Looking up at Mr. Jones, Sofie swallows the lump in her throat, takes a deep breath and says, "Thank you, Mr. Jones." Her gratitude shows on Sofie's face.

Mr. Jones simply says, "Don't mention it."

***

Mr. Jones helps Sofie out more than once that semester. The students fear him like God. He looks in on Sofie occasionally. Each time a reverent hush falls over the classroom. It is as if Jesus Christ just walked in.

Mr. Jones also brings in the Mothers' Club. Volunteer mothers of students come in with bright, new paper to cover the bulletin boards and double doors of the cupboards. He also tells the maintenance people to clean and polish Sofie's floor and repair or remove any broken furniture. He brings Sofie teacher's aides, adults that help in the classroom, for each of her classes. Mr. Jones even sets her free from her worst classes. He arranges substitutes to cover difficult classes, so she can observe other teachers' classes. When needed, Mr. Jones sends in counselors, assistant principals and once even the dean of students.

Mr. Jones knows that Sofie was thrown to the wolves, and like wolves, students sense fear, preying on their victims. He brings in the support Sofie needs as a first-year teacher. After all, thirty-five against one, the ratio of students to teachers, are not very good odds.

***

After lunch, Sofie figures only fourteen more flights of stairs to climb up and down before the end of the day. Three o'clock, that Friday afternoon comes none too soon. Sofie looks around her new classroom, dazed from the knees up and numb from the knees down.

I've got a lot of work to do to prepare for the week. Look over the textbooks; prepare five lessons for three subjects, grade pretests and record in the grade book. Oh yes! I'm buying some new low-heeled shoes tomorrow," Sofie vows to herself.

Wearily, Sofie piles up her little cart with her twenty pounds of stuff, signs out at the office, crawls into her old red Toyota and heads for home. In another two and a half hours amid the ribbons of red taillights on the freeway, at long last, she is home again.

CHAPTER 9

MRS. VIERMA?

What ever happened to Mrs. Vierma?" is the question usually asked after, "Are you a sub?" by the students in Sofie's science classes.

"I don't know. Whatever *did* happen to Mrs. Vierma?" Sofie responds to their question with the same question. After all, they were there last semester, not Sofie.

She inherited Mrs. Vierma's science classes, one hundred of the unruliest adolescents she ever encountered. Reports of Mrs. Vierma are as varied as the sources asked.

The official word from the administration is that Mrs. Vierma is out on disability and will not be returning. The principal and the four assistant principals are very vague about the cause or nature of Mrs. Vierma's disability. But, one thing is for certain, they are not talking about the episodes that went on in Mrs. Vierma's classroom.

The students knew better. They were there everyday to taunt Mrs. Vierma, to see what they could get away with. To see just how far they could push her until she went over the edge. It was like a game to them, and they were proud of the game. Some thought she might have died like the teacher they gave a heart attack. Others recounted the times Mrs. Vierma was yelling at them for one reason or another. Some recalled Mrs. Vierma's hands shaking so violently while trying to sip a bit of coffee from her cup, the magic liquid spilling over the rim. Still others talked about the drama of Mrs. Vierma, chasing one of the students around the room with a yardstick, screaming at the top of her lungs, *"SECURITY! SECURITY!"* Others told of

Mrs. Vierma's encounter with the over-sized eighth-grader, who punched her in the chest. Mrs. Vierma fell to the floor. The students thought that might have caused Mrs. Vierma to get breast cancer.

***

One day, Sofie asks her guardian angel, Mr. Jones, "Whatever *did* happen to Mrs. Vierma?"

"Mrs. Vierma? Why, she had a nervous breakdown," he says simply. "She was quite the nervous type, and just couldn't take it. She cracked."

"Oh yeah?" Sofie replies, worried she might be the next victim.

"Yeah, but hey...but don't let it get to you." He reassures Sofie. "If you have any trouble with any of those students, just send them down to me. I'll take care of them for you. Just hang in there. I know you can do it. These kids are just babies compared to where I taught my first year. Why, they had me in tears my first year more than once. It even drove me to drink. I lost my wife, the whole bit. But, hey, I got on the wagon, found a good woman who believed in me and turned it around. I know how tough it can be. That was a long time ago. This is my twenty seventh year of teaching and I love it. You'll love it too...once you get the hang of it. Keep them busy. Give them more work than they possibly can do in fifty minutes. Call their parents if they get out of line, and you'll do just fine."

***

With those words of encouragement and support, Sofie endures the students who sit in front and make faces at her. She tolerates the ones who heckle and talk back to her. She dodges the spitballs, paper clips, paper wads, and bits of erasers, even the ones who spit gum through the dismantled barrels of ballpoint pens. She breaks up fights between students. She calls the parents of the ones who talk constantly. She ignores those who beg, "Just one more chance, Ms. Rich, just one more chance." She even asks the mothers of four girls who talk constantly, to sit with them through one class

44

to keep them quiet. Those girls could have died from embarrassment, having their mothers there.

Even with all the help from Mr. Jones and others, the daily challenges of the classroom build up and take a toll on Sofie. Whenever it becomes just too much, she visits "Roomie-Zoomie," her old college roommate, for a sanity break.

CHAPTER 10

VISITS WITH ROOMIE-ZOOMIE

Roomie-Zoomie and Sofie have been friends ever since fate matched them up in the same dormitory room at the university. They were just nineteen years old, an eternity ago. Their friendship was forged together amid popcorn and soup during midnight study sessions and smoking cigars at frat parties. Once, the two roomies were erroneously accused of the infamous popcorn-based fire that broke out in the dorm. They were so naïve, and yet always getting into trouble for silliness. Silly things like staying out all night and sneaking boys into their room at the girls' dormitory. More than once they were grounded in their dorm room, except for classes and meals, for their alleged crimes.

Roomie-Zoomie (also known as RZ) and Sofie both dropped out of college to marry young within a year of each other. While married, they lived close to each other and within a year of each other, gave birth and raised two children each. Both divorced their first husbands and remarried. RZ was still married, but Sofie was now divorced from husband number two.

***

RZ is now a successful writer, living in the trendy Westside of Los Angeles. When things get too rough at John Quincy Junior High, Sofie seeks refuge in the companionship of her old collage friend. RZ is like the Red Cross

46

to Sofie, when she feels like a war battered soldier. The battleground being John Quincy in South-Central Los Angeles.

"What you need is some French pastries and strong coffee," RZ says in her soothing voice. RZ and Sofie walk over to the civilization of the local shopping mall. On the top floor of the mall is a cornucopia of eateries. The delicious aromas float through the food court among the tables of hungry, weary shoppers, resting their feet and filling their stomachs. The smell of fresh roast coffee and the most scrumptious, decadent French pastries Sofie ever laid eyes upon make her weep with happiness and forgetting the battles of the day.

"Now, you chose two and I'll chose two. My treat," RZ says touching Sofie's shoulder, nursing her back to mental health with the taste of sweets and coffee. Soon Sofie feels the stress of the week melting away with the aid of a sugar high and animated venting about the previous week's battles.

Sofie tells RZ about the 392 stairs she climbed one day just to change classrooms and classes. She tells RZ about all the industrious students engineering paper airplanes and other projectiles to launch in class at the moving target in front of the chalkboard. The target is of course, Sofie. She tells RZ about the artistry of the *KICK ME* signs some of the students create to stick on the backs of other students. Sofie also tells RZ about the guardian angel the administration sent to save her from the chaos and unruly students. She tells RZ all this and more. Every visit is a new episode to laugh and cry about.

After filled and fortified with sweets and coffee, RZ and Sofie stroll through the mall, surveying all the wonderful materiality in the windows of the trendiest shops. Even if she cannot not afford to buy anything on a first-year teacher's salary, she can still feast her eyes on such luxuries and pretend.

The two are so different, RZ and Sofie, yet the closest of friends. RZ is quiet and reserved, happily married, and writing adventures from her armchair. Sofie, on the other hand, is talkative, wild, and free. Impulsively changing careers and dancing on the edge, without a net. They are mirrored opposites, yet they could have been Siamese twins in another lifetime.

Then walking back to RZ's penthouse apartment, the two discuss the ills of today's society, and how to cure its infirmities.

47

Soon, they hug and bid farewell. Sofie heads home for the weekend to prepare for the next week's encounters with her students. Her simple goal now is to try to teach them something of science and math.

The drive home flies by swiftly at the late hour with not much traffic. Sofie's mind drifts back over two decades of friendship with Roomie-Zoomie. She feels so blessed, having such a good friend all these years.

CHAPTER 11

LEP KIDS AND THE RAISIN LAB

Sofie soon discovers why she is assigned teacher's aides in every class. All her students are LEP, Limited English Proficiency. What that means is these students cannot read or write English well. In most cases the only English these students hear in their home is from the cartoons on television. Assigning them anything to read or write is futile. They hate the science books, and only use them to tag gang logos in and throw about the classroom when the teacher isn't looking. Sofie finds books stuck behind bookcases, on top of cabinets and other hiding places. They don't want to be seen carrying books around or taking them home. Why? Because it is not macho to carry books. No self-respecting gang member would be caught dead carrying books home. To carry books or even do homework is to be called a "school boy," very unmacho.

Sofie wonders, *how can I get these students interested in science, if they can't even read English?*

A thought comes to Sofie: *Labs! That's it! To learn science, one must do science. They will all become my young scientists and we will do lots of labs.* Sofie picks up her teacher's edition of the physical science textbook and reads out loud from the back of the book. There, the Dancing Raisins Experiment is described:

"To get the students interested in the scientific process, try this little experiment. Soak raisins in water overnight, so that they plump up. Then drop in a small beaker of water and add one Alka-Seltzer tablet, and watch the raisins dance. The calcium carbonate molecules in the Alka-Seltzer will react with the hydrogen oxide molecules, releasing oxygen molecules that will cling to the water in the raisins, thus lifting the raisins to the surface of the water, so that they appear to jump around in the beaker."

Sounds easy enough for eighth grade LEP students. Sofie says to herself. On Sunday, she goes shopping for raisins and Alka-Seltzer in the name of science and education. Returning home again, she fills a glass half full of water, and dumps in the raisins. Watching the little glass of water with raisins, Sofie waits patiently for the raisins to plump up.

"What are you doing, Mom?" Justin asks, walking into the kitchen. He is puzzled, seeing his mother gazing into a glass of water on the counter.

"I am soaking raisins. I'm going to make them dance," Sofie answers with a straight face.

"Oh yeah? Let's see," Justin says grinning at his mother's attempt at raisin science.

"See Justin, by following the instructions in the textbook, I drop an Alka-Seltzer tablet into the water with the raisins in it and the raisins are supposed to dance."

Sofie and Justin wait. Nothing happens, other than the tablet fizzles itself out. The raisins lay lifeless on the bottom of the glass as still as before.

"Well, maybe the raisins need to soak a little longer." Sofie says in defense of her science experiment.

"Yeah, sure. Maybe the raisins are just too tired to dance," Justin says shaking his head then walking away in disbelief.

***

Monday morning, Sofie struts into her third-period science class, wearing her new red high-top sneakers.

"Nice shoes, Ms. Rich," Carlos yells out.

"Thanks," Sofie answers.

50

Then turning to her class, Sofie talks about science and being scientists. She is ready to wow them with her raisins and Alka-Seltzer trick, known in science as an experiment.

"Do you think raisins can dance?" She asks her LEP students.

"Dance?" questions Maria, the short girl with glasses, in the front row.

"Yeah, dance. You know, dance. Do you think they can dance?" Sofie taunts.

"No!" yells Carlos from the back of the class.

"Are you crazy?" asks Billy, a tall, lanky black boy who cannot sit still.

"Yeah, California Raisins, they can dance. I've seen them on TV. You know, the cartoon commercial for California Raisins," Lucy yells back, after putting away lipstick and eyeliner in her over-sized purse.

"Well, let's see," Sofie says, getting out her raisins and Alka-Seltzer. She has their attention now. "Today, you will all be scientists. Our question, called a theory, is 'Can raisins dance?' Some of you say, yes, they can. Some of you say, no, they can't. These are two different theories. We will test these theories using an experiment. We will put some raisins in a glass of water. Then we will drop this tablet into the water. We will observe the reaction and write down what we see. Then we will conclude which of the two theories about the ability of raisins to dance is correct. We will make observations and explain how the result of our experiment relates to the original question, 'Can raisins dance?' Shall we give it a try?"

Everyone gathers around to watch. Sofie has their interest. Out comes the beaker of water. Into the water, Sofie drops the well-soaked raisins. Next the Alka-Seltzer tablet is dropped. Everyone waits with great anticipation. Nothing happens. The raisins lay lifeless at the bottom of the beaker, a repeat performance from the night before. Disappointment and boos come from the future scientists. Sofie tries to explain what is supposed to happen. Then the bell rings, marking the end of the third-period.

Sofie sighs, "Oh well, I guess we must conclude the raisins cannot dance. But why? We'll give it a try fourth-period science class."

The bell rings again for the beginning of fourth-period. Her next science class is restless. Sofie asks the same question, "Do you think raisins can dance?"

"Dance?" She also gets the same reaction as third-period.

"Yeah, *dance*," she says, baiting them with the question. "Dance, you know, dance. Do you think they can dance? Maybe if they hear the right music, do you think that raisins can dance?"

Jimmy starts humming a little rap music. Sofie starts softly singing, "Heard it through the Grapevine," as she gathers the students around her. She brings back the beaker of water, the presoaked raisins and the magic tablet of Alka-Seltzer. She goes through her speech about science and scientists. She starts the experiment. Again, nothing happens.

Just then, Sofie glances toward the door and sees Manuel, a small Latino boy with sad eyes, over by the door. He has a dark blue felt tipped marker in his hand and he is writing his gang logo on the wall and door!

"Hey you!" She shouts at Manuel. "What do you think you are doing? Are you writing on my door?" Dashing over to the doorway, she catches Manuel red handed, tagging her classroom, marker in hand.

"What?" Manuel asks, innocently. "I ain't doin' nothin'."

"You're writing on my walls," Sofie says, eyes blazing. "I saw you with my own eyes. What's that in your hand? A marker. You have a marker in your hand, and you just marked up my walls with it."

"No, I didn't," denying the act with a straight face.

"Manuel, I saw you. Don't try to deny it," insists Sofie. "You're going down to the Deans Office." Sofie can feel the rage welling up in her body. Her heart pounding, face flushed and stomach churning, she knows what she must do. In her heart, she wonders why this junior high school must be such a battleground.

"No! Please no, Ms. Rich," Manuel now pleads. "Just one more chance, Ms. Rich. Just one more chance."

Furious, she grabs Manuel by the shoulder, holding him until the lunch bell rings. When all the students leave for lunch, Sofie closes the classroom door and calls Mr. Rodriguez, the Dean of Students. The middle-aged, stocky man, with a thick head of curly black hair and weathered, wrinkled skin, enters the room.

Sofie recaps the incident. "Mr. Rodriguez, Manuel was over there by the door, tagging the wall and door with this marker," holding up the dark blue marker, "while the rest of the class was involved in a science experiment."

Mr. Rodriguez turns to Manuel and looks down on the small boy, saying, "Is that true, Manuel?"

"Naw, man, I didn't do it," he lies.

"What?!" exclaims Sofie in disbelief. "I *saw* him marking the walls with my own eyes! He still had the marker in his hand when I caught him!"

"Well Manuel, I guess we will have to call your mother for a little chat," Mr. Rodriguez says calmly. "A parent-teacher conference is in order."

Students gather outside the doorway looking in to see what's happening. They freeze, glaring at Manuel Salazar, "wannabe" gang-tagger, as he is escorted to the dreaded detention office by the Dean of Students.

Later, during the parent-teacher conference, Manuel Salazar, denies the tagging, claiming that the marks were already there. Sofie insists she saw him with her own eyes. He is found guilty as charged, to his mother's dismay. For the rest of the semester, Sofie must report his behavior in class on a daily progress report.

By the time sixth-period science class comes around, Sofie wearily tries the Dancing Raisins experiment one more time. God smiles down on Sofie this time, and the raisins dance. They dance for her sixth-period science class, and the kids all cheer.

CHAPTER 12

OVERNIGHTS
WITH MOM

The eventual success of the Dancing Raisins Lab is the turning point for Sofie's teaching career. Educating junior high school students is a dance indeed, even if you do it with raisins. Sofie finally captures the students' curiosity and turns book learning into discovering the magic of science.

But even with her newly-found success, Sofie is obliged to take six more units of earth science classes to renew her teaching contract with John Quincy Junior High School. The good news is that the school district offers the classes free to teachers and pays the teachers to take the classes. The bad news, Sofie must get up at 4:30 AM, get on the freeway by 5:30 AM, get to school by 7:00 AM, to get a spot in the school parking lot. After teaching five classes, leaving at 3:00 PM, she must drive to Hollywood two nights a week and sit in class until 7:30 PM. However, class never seems to let out on time. There is always a question Sofie needs answered about teaching her physical science classes. Patiently, she waits her turn to talk to the instructor. By the time her day is over, she feels like road-kill, crushed and lifeless. She wonders how keep her eyes open for the drive home. But she is there faithfully every Tuesday and Wednesday night.

To ease the stress of it all, on those long days she has class, Sofie spends the night at her mother's house in Glenoaks. Winding back through the side streets of her old neighborhood brings back images of her childhood.

She sees the ancient Lutheran church she attended with her two brothers and parents. Driving down the street, her eye catches the pastrami stand still on that far corner. Over there, the big brown apartment building remains towering three stories. Sofie remembers passing it while riding around the block on her first bike. And there is the neighborhood market she walked to as a child to buy milk or bread. Where is it now? Gone. Replaced by a discount tire store. There to the left is McArthur Park, it was called Westlake Park when she was a child. But oh, how the surrounding area around the park has changed. No more Jewish bakeries and eateries. Instead, many little Latino shops and even the magnificent movie theater she and her brothers frequented, transformed into a giant swap meet. *How sad*, Sofie ponders.

She drives along the bus routes she used to take to get to church in Los Angeles, after her family moved to Glenoaks. Sofie had not finished her confirmation classes, so she took the bus into Los Angeles on Saturday morning, transferring two times and taking hours. She was only eleven years old, but there was nothing to fear back then.

Arriving at her mother's house late at night, Sofie bubbles over with stories of the day. Her mother's huge house with four bedrooms, and two baths, sits on a hill with a view of the mountains. Her terraced garden, where she grows every botanical species imaginable, goes all the way up to the next street.

Greeting her mother with a big hug and a warm smile, Sofie feels the comfort of a baby bird coming home to the childhood nest.

No matter how long it takes driving to Mom's house, dinner is always waiting. Walking through the front door, Sofie smells the delicious aromas of food keeping warm in the oven. A complete meal of meat, potatoes, two vegetables, a garden salad, sometimes soup, hot coffee, and dessert. All for Sofie, just like when she was a kid. Sometimes Sofie arrives early and her mom takes her to the local Swedish Smorgasbord. There they can eat as much as they want. With so many choices, Sofie samples some of everything and always three desserts to sweeten the evening.

In the morning, her mom makes a breakfast of freshly squeezed orange juice, hot oatmeal with raisins (non-dancing raisins) and brown sugar, hot coffee and toast topped with homemade jelly, just like when Sofie was a kid.

Her mom packs a lunch for Sofie to take. In the brown paper bag are two sandwiches, carrot sticks, celery stocks with peanut butter in the grove, an apple cored and cut into quarters, and homemade chocolate chip cookies, just like when she was a kid. Nothing has changed. She is still her mama's little girl, even though she is full-grown and a mother herself. Stress from her hectic pace is the only thing preventing Sofie from gaining fifty pounds between RZ's pastries and her mama's meals.

In the evening, Sofie narrates the day's events, the victories and defeats of each class, and the encounters with each of her livelier students. Her mom is a great audience. She listens intently to Sofie's every word, sometimes offering advice, other times laughing along with her daughter. Still other times her mom voices concerns.

"What about that teacher you replaced, that Mrs. Vierma? Did you ever find out what happened to her?" Mom asks.

"I don't know, really. I've heard several stories from different sources. Nearest I can figure, she just did not show up in school one day. The kids had substitute teachers ever since. I am their first permanent teacher since November of last year."

Mom takes Sofie's hand in hers and says, "I'm praying for you." From the time Sofie leaves for school, until safe at home, she knows she is in God's hands and no harm will befall her. Sofie and her mother grow very close during that semester of teaching in the inner city of Los Angeles.

In the morning after breakfast, Sofie gathers up her books, lunch, and any other goodies her mother loads her up with. No one ever leaves her mother's house empty handed. "What can I give you?" Mom always says. Whether it is a jar of her homemade boysenberry jelly from her homegrown berry patch, or an assortment of groceries she bought doubles of since they were on sale, Mom always has a bag of goodies for departing guests.

Sofie and her mom walk down the long flight of stairs to the street below to Sofie's old Toyota. With a clean rag, Sofie's mom wipes off the fog gathered on the windshield overnight. A wave good bye and a toot-toot of her horn, Sofie is ready to start another day of teaching at John Quincy Junior High.

Getting on the freeway for just a short distance, Sofie takes the China-town off-ramp and drives in through the downtown district to her school. The streets are all but empty, shops not open yet at that early hour. Driving past the Los Angeles architecture of so long ago, again Sofie recalls memo-ries in her mind. *There is City Hall, just like it was in Dragnet on television. And Grand Central Market, where my mother, shopped for the week's fruits and vegetables. She carried six shopping bags, three in each hand. One bag just for ten pounds of oranges that she later juiced by hand. I remember holding on to Mom's skirt with a tight grip in a sea of knees, afraid to let go, afraid of getting lost, never to see my mother again, in such a large market with so many people.*

"Is that Angel's Flight on the block I just passed?" Sofie says out loud. "And where did all those high-rises come from over the Third Street Tunnel? What did they do to Pershing Square?" looking at the purple, square tower, shocking pink columns and bright yellow ochre walls. "It sure doesn't look like I remember from my childhood." *Nothing changes and yet everything changes.* Soon she reaches her school in half the time it takes driving from South Orange County.

Staying with her mother seems like the perfect solution to cut the com-muting time, but nothing is perfect in this imperfect world. One of the draw-backs to staying at her mother's house during the week is that she enjoys the time talking and eating, but there is no time to get any schoolwork done. As a result, her weekends are consumed with tons of papers to grade and lessons to plan. Sofie lives the life of a nun, no social life at all. This is not all bad, as it gives her time to heal the wounds of a broken heart from her last relationship.

Summer is coming, and she has six weeks off to catch up on her social life. *Hooray!*

CHAPTER 13

FIELD TRIP QUEEN AND BILLY

By mid-semester, Sofie earns a level of respect from her students through lots of labs and field trips. The first field trip Sofie arranges is a trip to the Museum of Science and Industry. Upon seeing her, students nod or call out, "Hey, Ms. Rich," from across the campus. Sofie lines up several more field trips, and now she is known as the Field Trip Queen. Her prerequisite for field trips are passing grades and good behavior. For some students, the latter being the hardest to achieve.

Billy is one. The tall, lanky black student, who always wears jeans, a white tee shirt, and sneakers. He cannot stay seated for more than five minutes at a time. Born a drug baby, his mother was on heroin when she carried him in her womb. Billy is constantly fidgeting with his pencil or pen or drumming his fingers on the desk. He always has an excuse why he is out of his seat, getting a pen, sharpening a pencil, telling someone something, the list is endless. His mood swings go from silly to depressed, along with the constant moving and talking behavior. He only speaks in one volume, *loud,* whether he is yelling or laughing or sometimes even crying. His anger comes as swiftly as his appeals for, "Just one more chance, Ms. Rich. Just one more chance." If anyone looks at Billy the wrong way, his paranoia lashes out in anger or fear.

One day, in desperation, Sofie Richmond takes Billy aside and says to him, "Maybe we should call your mom, Billy, and have her sit with you in class. You know, like those four girls who talked too much last week?"

"Don't live with my mom," Billy says, fidgeting again, eyes shifting back and forth.

"You don't?"

"No. I don't," Billy, confesses. "I don't live with my mom. I live with my cousin." There is sadness in Billy's voice as if fighting back the urge to cry.

"Billy, why don't you live with your mother," Sofie asks, puzzled by his reply.

"Mom's on drugs," Billy fires back, now angry. "I live with my cousin. He's an adult. He's thirty."

"What about your dad, Billy." Sofie inquires, feeling sadness for the boy welling up inside her. *What happens to the families of the inner-city children?*

"My dad's dead," Billy states flatly. "My dad's dead. My mom is on drugs, and I live with my cousin."

Billy is just one of the lost children in this never-never land. Life is so hard out there in the gangland neighborhoods, the children come to school to be with their friends, because it is safe. No drugs, no violence, campus police to keep it safe. They do not come to school to learn, they come to school to play in relative peace.

CHAPTER 14

FIRE!

S ofie, the newly crowned Field Trip Queen, just has arranged a plum of a field trip to the Griffith Park Observatory and Planetarium. Inside the observatory are numerous exhibits of planets in our solar system and laws of physics. In addition to the exhibits, the observatory has two huge telescopes aimed at different planets, moons, or stars that students can view. There is even a laser light show on black holes in space.

The field trip includes transportation by the district's school bus and lunch afterwards in Travel Town, a collection of old passenger and freight trains. The students can climb aboard the real old locomotives to get a good look of the technology of the past modes of transportation. To the students, the best part of the field trip is missing a whole day of classes. To Sofie, the best part of the trip is taking her students on an adventure outside the classroom and opening their minds to new experiences.

But this time, there is a problem. Sofie can only take thirty students to the observatory, and she has one hundred and eight students in her three science classes. Only the best students from each class will go.

As Sofie begins announcing who gets the coveted trip slips for the Observatory Field Trip, the students huddle around, crowding in on her. Then suddenly, from across the room she sees a flash of light. Someone yells, "FIRE!"

The wastepaper basket by the door is ablaze! Mayhem brakes out. Students are everywhere but in their seats, screaming and yelling. While attention is diverted to the flames, Billy is running toward the bellowing smoky fire, fearlessly dumping the contents of the wastepaper basket on the floor and stomping out the blaze. Cinders and ashes fly everywhere. Heroically, Billy smothers the fire, leaving just the stench of burnt paper and plastic in the air.

Sofie's brain is churning, *this must be the worst nightmare I ever had, and I will awaken any moment. Wrong. These are south-central junior high school students, with nothing to lose. What or who ever made me think I can teach these students math or science? This is insane. This would never happen in an accounting department. I gave up accounting for this? What am I doing here? Am I crazy? What am I to do?* Her mind is racing between flight and fight.

Suddenly, the lunch bell rings. Sofie runs for one door, instructing the aide to cover the other door. "No one leaves, until we find out who set the fire!" Sofie yells. She holds the class captive and sends out a trustworthy student to summon Mr. Ortega, the Dean of Discipline, and the campus police. The dean arrives with two police officers.

"What's going on here?" Dean Ortega demands in a voice that means, 'You lie, you die.' The dean, a short, stocky, muscular, middle-aged man, looks strong enough to fight his way out of a bar room brawl. He is tough, and the students know he means business. The dean has the power of assigning twenty hours of detention, campus clean up duty, suspension from school, transfer to another school, or even expulsion out of the entire school district. No one messes with the dean. He has ways of getting to the truth.

The whole class starts talking at once. Little Jimmy shouts out, "Someone walked by the open door and threw a lighted match in the wastebasket, yelling, 'Death to the KBG.'"

Big Mike jumps out of his seat and claims in a deep voice, "Don't look at me. It ain't me. I didn't do it!"

Gerald stares down at his shoes through his thick black framed glasses and says casually, "Maybe spontaneous combustion?"

"*QUIET!*" yells Dean Ortega. The whole room falls silent. Turning to Sofie, he asks in a voice only a few decibels lower, "What happened here, Ms. Richmond?"

Sofie, feeling her heart pounding in her chest, searches for the words to explain the chaos. "Well, you see Dean..." she says, trying to keep her voice

61

steady as all eyes are on her. Silence permeates the room in the heat of the afternoon. The musky smell of thirty-two nervous adolescents fills the air. "...It was like this. I was just about to announce who in the class will get the trip slips for the upcoming field trip to the Griffith Park Observatory, when I glance over to the door and see fire. The whole corner of the room by the door is ablaze." Sofie then takes a deep breath, holds it for a second, then lets the air out slowly. Gaining her composure, she says to Dean Ortega in a low, steady voice, "No one from outside started the fire. It was someone in this classroom." As soon as those words leave her lips, the room buzzes with denials.

"*Quiet!*" Again, Dean Ortega yells. "No one is leaving for lunch until I find out who did it!" Then turning to Sofie again says, "Ms. Richmond, you can go and eat your lunch. You don't need to stay any longer." Shocked, Sofie leaves the classroom while Dean Ortega holds and interrogates the whole class until the guilty person is nailed.

The *girl* who set the fire is booted out of the entire school district for arson. Sofie never found out why *Marta* set the fire. Maybe her grades were so low...hard to say why.

Later, students come up to Sofie to taunt her, asking, "Did they burn your room down, Ms. Rich?"

"I heard they set fire to your classroom, Ms. Rich."

"Fire! Did I scare you, Ms. Rich?"

Billy is granted a trip slip for the field trip to the Observatory. Even though he is failing the class, Sofie still lets Billy go for his extraordinary bravery in putting out the fire in the room.

***

And what a great field trip it is. The students load into the bus, while the bus driver cautions Sofie to keep the windows at least halfway up. "Last year there was a shooting at this very corner," he says, showing Sofie the dozens of bullet holes in the side of the bus. "We don't want anyone to get hurt on this trip."

So, the science students on field trip kept their windows up and the music down and soon they are on their way. Sofie sees the cares of the outside world and the stress of the classrooms melting away from her students. As they kick back in the old yellow school bus, big smiles spread across their contented faces, and Sofie's face, too. At long, long last, they are on their way.

CHAPTER 15
CINCO DE MAYO

Teaching in Los Angeles does have its sane moments. Cinco de Mayo, the 5th of May, is one of them. The school population is ninety-five percent Hispanic, mainly from Mexico, although a good number are from Central America. So, Mexico's Independence Day is cause for celebration.

Mrs. Perez, the assistant principal in charge of text books, field trips and special events, goes all out for Cinco de Mayo. She organizes contests, prizes for posters, and essays on the theme, "What does Cinco de Mayo Mean to Me?" The story of the Mexican Revolution and the winning essay is read over the intercom in English, as well as Spanish, for all to hear. The campus quad outside is decorated from stem to stern with brightly colored crape paper in Mexico's colors of red, white, and green. A five-man mariachi band is hired for the noontime festivities. Best of all is the special assembly held on Cinco de Mayo.

The students love assemblies of any kind, because it is a chance to get out of class and kick back. Lining up her students in two straight lines, Sofie threatens, "We are not leaving until everyone is silent."

"Hush, Luis!" Lupe hisses at the chattering boy behind her in line.

"Hush, yourself!" Luis fires back.

"Shhhh!" Maria whispers loudly to Luis.

"Shut up!" Danny hollers.

"You shut up, or I'll shut you up!" Jessie chides back.

"Oh yeah? Do you want to fight about it?" Danny says, ready to jump Jesse.

Stepping up to the hot-headed boys ready to fight, Sofie glares at them says, "Now, you two, do you want to go to detention, or do you want to go the assembly?"

"No, Ms. Rich. No. We'll be good."

"Okay, then..."

Then looking at the faces of her other students, Sofie whispers, "The rest of you, chill out and be quiet, or we are not going anywhere."

When it is finally quiet, Sofie marches her junior soldiers to the back of the auditorium, where they enter the enormous hall in perfect formation. Mr. Griswold, one of the assistant principals at the top of the stairs going into the auditorium, nods his approval, then directs Sofie to one of the three doors to enter. Down the aisle of the huge theater-sized room they march in perfectly silent order. Sofie walks next to the worst offenders to discourage any improper behavior. She wants to see the assembly, too. Filling in two rows of seats, the students sit down, while Sofie stands. Looking over her class, she can tell those students prone to talk. She shuffles the talkers around either near to her on the end of the row or next to a student of the opposite sex, who hates him or her. She promises the next move being out the door. Sofie can quiet a student with just a dirty look. *Yes, I'm getting the hang of this teaching business*, she thinks to herself.

Soon Mrs. Perez comes out on stage and gives the flag salute and reads the agenda. She introduces Mrs. Castillo, the principal, who says a few words in English and in Spanish about Cinco de Mayo. Then the drama class does a rendition of the Mexican legend of Creation.

Next on the Cinco de Mayo program comes the long awaited Mexican flamenco dancers in costumes of full skirts decorated with brightly colored ribbons. Whirling and twirling, the dancers spin colorful patterns on the stage. Then the men come out in their tight black pants, little bolero jackets, and big sombreros, pounding out the rhythm of the music with their black boots. The students cheer at the sights and sounds of the flamenco dancers. They love it. At the end of the assembly, the students are invited to come down in front of the stage to dance to the lively Latin music. Latino students pour from their seats into the area in front of the stage. Bouncing and bobbing to the melodies, they are in their element and loving every minute of it.

At lunch, the school menu is a feast of Mexican delights. Tacos, burritos, enchiladas, and of course, refried beans and Spanish rice, all sprinkled with spicy salsa. The generously spiced food brings tears to Sofie's eyes and sniffles to her nose. Mariachi musicians appear on the second-story balcony of the science building. They serenade the students with trumpets and guitars, while the Latino students dance below in the quad, joined by the flamenco dancers from the assembly performance.

"Come on, Ms. Rich, dance with us." Some of Sofie's students are urging. "You can do it."

"Yeah, like those raisins in the fizzy water!"

"I don't know how," Sofie says.

"It's easy. We'll show you," answers Julio, and demonstrates his moves. *The student is now teaching the teacher. That's an interesting turn around,* Sofie thinks. She throws up her hands and gives it a whirl. She may look foolish, but she doesn't care. That afternoon, Sofie is one with her students. She dances.

Word spreads. Sofie's students now come up to her saying, "You were dancing, weren't you Ms. Rich?"

"I saw you!"

"Our club is having a party, Ms. Rich, want to come?"

Being a teacher at John Quincy Junior High School is like living in a small village. Everyone knows your business. Sofie smiles to herself to think, her students witness her acting like just another human being.

CHAPTER 16

BLOSSOMING INTO SWANHOOD

One thing becomes clear, these children in South-Central Los Angeles are no different than any other children anywhere else. They are all going through their hormonal changes, all dealing with their insecurities in one way or another. They are all trying to find themselves in this world, to cope with the uncertainties of the future.

The differences are also apparent to those who dare to come close enough to look. The Hispanic culture is very different from the Anglo culture. In many ways, some Hispanic children are less mature than some of their counterparts in the Anglo culture. Living far simpler lives, sometimes ten to a household with multiple generations of relations, they are more playful, the girls giving teddy bears and candy to each other for birthdays, the boys dominating the basketball courts at noon. They cling to each other for protection against the hostile world that they live in, forming gangs that are surrogate families to them. Most have no idea what they will be doing five years into the future. The ones who see a future want to be in law enforcement, perhaps the police are their only positive role models and what they see the most.

The other strong influence in their young lives is the Catholic Church. As in their native land, most go to Mass at least once a week, some sing in the choir, most are baptized and confirmed in the Catholic Church. They are a deeply religious people. God is with them through all their hardships.

These are students coming of age, girls look forward to their fifteenth birthday celebration, much like a debutante ball. The girls struggle daily with the role model of the Virgin Mary and the machismo boys trying to romance them into sexual encounters. At fifteen, girls are considered women. Many marry and get pregnant at sixteen, not able to use contraceptives because of the teachings of the Church. It is difficult to resist the charms of their Latino boyfriends. To graduate from junior high in ninth grade is a great achievement. College is an impossible dream.

The Latino boys have their own body language and style. In the seventh grade, they are playful children. In the eighth grade, their hormones take over and they will stare dreamy-eyed at any girl who has started to bud breasts and reveal cleavage. Eighth grade is the time that the "wannabe" gang members take on the appearance of their gangs. The weird hair styles, like buzz cut except for a tail at the back of the neck. Or buzzed short on the sides with a river of straight black hair cascading from the forehead back. These haircuts are some trademarks of different gangs in the neighborhood. The baggy pants, size 42 on a size 12 frame, denotes tagging crewmembers. The unhemmed, oversize jeans, fringed at the bottom, slit to the ankle, indicates another affiliation. Gang clothing or colors were prohibited on campus, so many of the students with unhemmed jeans ask to use Sofie's stapler, to staple their pant hems up while in school. After school, they rip the staples out of their pant hems to hang with their homeboys, then staple them back again the next day in school.

By the ninth grade, the boys are well into their manliness. They master the swagger of leading with their shoulders, elbows out, ready to swing a punch at any given moment. They develop a threatening stare, without blinking to intimidate their enemies. They now know how to kick back against walls and glare at passersby.

All these outward signs of their version of manhood are learned by the ninth grade. But they have not learned their multiplication tables, and they have not learned their fractions, and they have not mastered the English language.

The Latino boys are very clever at diverting attention away from their illiteracy. They use their charm and charisma. Once Sofie is sent to observe an ESL (English as a Second Language) class and learn from another teacher how to reach and teach this type of student. As she enters the classroom, she notices all the students in the class are in a constant state of motion and chatter. It is as if the Creator sprinkled some spicy Latin language onto this mixture of colorful children and is in the process of stirring up all the ingredients to make the class special. The instant Sofie enters the room, all motion and noises stop. All eyes are diverted to her, the only Anglo in the room. Although they spoke no English, Sofie can tell the question on all their young minds. *Who is this strange redheaded woman? Why is she here?* The children are drawn to Sofie, like she is some giant magnet. They are curious, to say the least. As Sofie walks to the back of the room where the other teacher's desk is located, their gazes trail after her. She is an oddity to the Hispanic students in the room.

"I'm Ms. Richmond, a new teacher here," Sofie says, introducing herself to the ESL teacher, Mrs. Hernandez. "I've been sent to your classroom to observe your class, and your teaching methods. Is that all right with you?" she asks nervously.

"Sure," says Mrs. Hernandez meekly. "Sit back here."

Sofie does as she is told and sits at the back of the class, watching and listening. As class begins, one young man cannot keep his eyes off Sofie. He stares at her for quite a while, and then raises his eyebrows two times with a smile. In the time-tested tradition of monkey see, monkey do, Sofie raises her eyebrows two times also and smiles back at the young student. She thinks nothing of the gesture, sure that it is only a harmless nod of acquaintance.

Surprised and delighted, the student raises his eyebrows and smiles back again, and then again.

Sofie thinks, *it must be some sort of game,* and so again she mimics the Latino boy with eyebrows raises two times and a smile.

Now this ESL student brings his friends over to show them the response he receives. Again, the eyebrows and the smile routine are performed.

Again, Sofie responds in kind, thinking to herself, *how cute and childlike these ESL junior high school students are?*

Mrs. Hernandez, seeing the disturbance, brings an end to it. In Spanish, she tells the class of mischievous students, "Okay class, that's enough. Get back to your seats and start on your assignment for today. You only have twenty minutes to finish or it will be homework tonight." The class settles down, eyes returning to the handouts on their desk, only sneaking a quick glance at Sofie for the rest of the period.

Later, in the halls or on campus, whenever that certain ESL student sees Sofie, he raises his eyebrows two times with a smile, and gets his buddies to do the same.

Weeks go by, and then one day over lunch with Mr. Martinez, another ESL teacher, Sofie tells her story of the eyebrows and the smile. Mr. Martinez just laughs. "Do you know what it means when a Latin male raises his eyebrows two times and smiles to a woman, and the woman does the same gesture back?" he asks Sofie.

"No. What?" Sofie replies, puzzled. It had not occurred to her that there is even a meaning behind the gesture.

Mr. Martinez laughs again, and says, "When a man in the Latin culture raises his eyebrows two times and smiles, it means, '*How about it!*' It, meaning sex. When the woman raises her eyebrows two times and smiles back to the man, it means, '*You're on! Yes, I will go to bed with you.*' That student must think you're pretty hot stuff, and he is going to get laid by the redheaded teacher!" Mr. Martinez explains the custom, his bulging eyes try to hold back his laughter.

Sofie stares open-mouthed at Mr. Martinez and they both break out laughing. Mr. Martinez laughs at the naiveté of Sofie and the absurdity of it all. They both laugh and laugh until their sides hurt.

CHAPTER 17

ALGEBRA ANTICS

You laugh a lot when you are a teacher. It keeps you from crying, or worst yet, loosing what sanity you have left, like Mrs. Vierma. The case in point is Sofie's ninth-grade Algebra 1B class. Two-thirds of the class failed the Algebra 1A, or passed with a D the semester before when taught by another teacher.

The girls who are failing are very much into talking and putting on make-up to pass the time. Most of the girls just open their purse, take out their mirrors and gaze into them, perhaps asking "Who's the fairest?" Not getting the right answer, they take lipstick, mascara, and eye shadow out of their purses, and begin to apply the wonder products. That is, most girls, except for Nina. Nina has a whole toolbox full of cosmetics she carries with her all day. In fact, this box, chuck full of miracle remedies, is more important to her than her books, which she sometimes forgets to bring to class. Nina sits in the back of the room during Sofie's fifth-period Algebra class. She not only studies and remedies her own face but also the faces of other girls in class. Finding any repairable flaw, she opens her box of tricks and brings out the tools to correct the situation. Out of the box, come tweezers, lipliner, eyeliner, eyeshadow, mascara, and the latest shade of lipstick, blue-black red. With the hand of an artist, she tweezes, lines, and colors her clients, while Sofie tries desperately to teach linear equations and polynomials. After all, one must be beautified, ready for the encounters with the opposite sex after school.

The boys, many of whom are failing, are very much into ditching, drawing, sleeping, or causing disturbances to distract Sofie's attention away from the day's lesson. Some boys, the few who show up for class, use a combination of activities, including tattooing sleeping students in class with ballpoint pens. The best at distraction are Raymond and Jessie, two Latinos who are over six feet tall and sprouting facial hair. The rest of the students come to class just to see what Raymond and Jessie will do that day. Each day is a new antic.

One steamy afternoon, Raymond and Jessie are snickering in the back row. While Sofie is writing $X = 2Y + 20$ *and* $Y = 5X - 10$, Raymond and Jessie get up out of their seats and start parading around the room. They hold up signs made for all to see, with hearts and flowers surrounding the words *DELIA LOVES JUAN!!* For the record, Delia is the prettiest girl in the Algebra class, who is now blushing under her perfect make-up, applied by Nina. And Juan, although he is the smartest boy in class, he is only five feet tall and overweight, with an overdose of acne on his oily face. Not much classwork is done that day, until Sofie sends Raymond and Jessie to the detention room.

Raymond and Jessie are always in detention unless they are dropping acid or sleeping in the back of the room. Trying to learn algebra is a painful reminder of how much they do not know. Neither boy knows multiplication tables, division, or fractions. Yet the principal insists all ninth-graders must take Algebra. For Raymond and Jessie, it is easier to get kicked out of class and zone out in detention than to sit through hours of meaningless classroom lectures.

Sofie is successful only a few times getting the two boys to drop by after school for some tutoring. They will work problems on the board when no one is around to see them learning. After all, they have a reputation to uphold. They do not want to be known as "schoolboys," boys who *like* school. Those days, when they stop by for tutoring, are the days they have nowhere else to go after school. Sometimes they are kicked out of their own homes by a step-dad or beaten by an uncle they live with. For Raymond and Jessie, drugs are a means of escape from the turmoil of their world. Drugs are their savior.

Then one day, close to the end of Sofie's first semester, Raymond and Jessie do not show up for class at all. Instead, there is a drop slip for each boy in her office mailbox, along with the bulletin and other assorted school papers. Staring at the drop slips in her hand, Sofie feels sadness deep in her heart for those two lost boys. Raymond and Jessie are caught with drugs and expelled from school.

Sofie agonizes over the lost students. If only she could have taught them to dance to the rhythm of Algebra and Mathematics, like those soaked raisins in the fizzy water. If only she could have soaked them full of knowledge and added a little excitement like the Alka-Seltzer tablet to the water to make the raisins dance. She shakes her head.

But Raymond and Jessie just slipped through one of the cracks of the educational institution called John Quincy Junior High School. Sofie fights back her tears, as she prays silently for their future.

CHAPTER 18

OFF TRACK!

With the end of the semester in sight, Sofie looks forward to the reward for her victories and for endurance of her defeats. The reward, which is the same for the students, is the summer off! Sofie starts counting the days, just like the students she is teaching.

Tired and exhausted, at long, long last, she completes her first semester. Once off track, she has time to reflect on the events of her first semester.

***

On the first day, she was totally unprepared and naïve. She was given a room on the third floor to teach classes in math, homeroom, science 9, physical science, and algebra. The students were totally wild and out of control after having four substitutes in four days. The question, "What ever happened to Mrs. Vierma?" came up time and time again. The worst time was her second day of switching classes and rooms. She had to trudge up and down four flights of stairs, eight times in one day in high heel shoes just to walk her students to each class. One minor victory that day, keeping most of the students from leaning out of the window of her third story classroom. And no one jumped.

Then everything was going well, she thought, *until the fire. That was the all-time low point in my teaching career.* The girl who tried to set fire to the classroom by torching the wastepaper basket. Marta, the arsonist, was expelled.

Another low point popping into Sofie's consciousness was the six-inch switch blade knife found on her classroom floor one day. The knife was not, in any stretch of the imagination, standard school supplies. It was more along the lines of a lethal weapon.

How could she forget the shooting across the street in the small neighborhood convenience store? One of the students from John Quincy shot the owner, and last she heard, the owner was in intensive care at Los Angeles General Hospital.

Nor could she forget the story of the girl who was stabbed to death by someone's mother over a drug deal.

And of course the fights, the worst being the fight that broke out between two Latino girls over a boyfriend during Sofie's last field trip. Yes, Sofie certainly had a rough start in teaching.

But hey, she survived her first semester. Sofie being an optimist, preferred to focus on her victories. Victories like making raisins dance with a little help from an Alka-Seltzer tablet. And not to forget the bubble gum labs, a means of measuring the sugar content in bubble gum by weighing the gum before and after chewing, to find the difference in weight. Victories like being the newly crowned Field Trip Queen. Organizing student field trips to the Museum of Science and Industry, the Griffith Park Observatory, and Travel Town. Best of all, the trip to the McDonnell Douglas Space Station Mock-up, where the students got to explore it up close and personal.

***

Sofie sits at her desk, looking back at all the referrals, a whole drawer full, and all the parent conferences. Thumbing through some of the referrals, she reflects on the times she kept the noisy students in at lunch. Maybe, just maybe she made a bit of a difference.

She smiles, feeling a warm sense of pride. Looking around her room, her heart swells as she thinks of all the help and encouragement from her mentor teacher, Mr. Jones, and others who helped her out.

Feeling weepy, she touches the red ink pen she used to sign all the yearbooks and remembers all the hugs from her ninth-graders at the end of the year.

Now summer is here and Sofie feels the rush of euphoria flood over her like an ocean wave. She realizes she is finally off track!!!

CHAPTER 19

BACK IN THE TRENCHES

The teacher's reward for months of standing in front of thirty or more students every hour, five times a day, as a moving target while trying to teach is the summer off. *Yes, it is well worth grading papers till one o'clock in the morning to get the final grades in for the end of the semester and to get three glorious months of summer vacation.* Sofie has the whole summer to do whatever, or go wherever, she wanted.

The only problem with all that freedom is the reality shock of going back into the trenches in the fall. Sofie must return to John Quincy Junior High School. She signed a contract for a whole year. And now, in only two short weeks, she is expected to be in front of five classrooms of junior high school students, fully prepared to teach five subjects she has never taught before, plus homeroom.

Sofie sighs as the panic sets in. Even before she arrived home from her four-week vacation traveling around the country on Amtrak, she questions her sanity.

"Why did I sign up for a second semester? Truth be told, the students at John Quincy Junior High are more interested in tagging walls, fighting, applying cosmetics, and setting fires in classrooms than learning math or science," Sofie rationalizes out loud.

"Sure, the teens on the train I traveled on were drawn to me. Even the most bothersome ones I got to work the math puzzles I handed out. And it *was* fun to listen to their insatiable chatter about everything and anything that mattered in their young lives. But teach for another eighteen weeks, with two hundred and thirty-five students in five classes a day? Am I crazy?" she wonders. *Too late. I signed a contract.*

When Sofie returns home, the panicky feeling intensifies. A paralyzing fear consumes her. She must prepare lessons for all her new classes. Classes she's never taught before.

She surveys the situation. "Let's see. I have two classes of marine science, with thirty students in each class. I have no textbooks for the marine science, only fourteen reference books on seashells. My physical science class covers the earth sciences of geology, mineralogy, meteorology, and space science, all subjects I never studied, let alone taught. Physical science does have textbooks. How am I expected to know what to teach? Even the two classes of mathematics are different from the two I taught the semester before. One is eighth-grade math and the other was a combination of seventh, eighth, and ninth grade ESL (English as a Second Language) math classes. The students do not speak or understand English and some are illiterate in Spanish as well. Some students only have one or two years of formal schooling. A lot of the students in the ESL math combo class are from the rural areas of Mexico or Central America, and do not have much schooling at all, let alone math."

Sofie decides to teach the ESL students from the eighth-grade math textbook. Doing so, she need only prepare for three subjects instead of four. All the lesson plans Sofie prepared last semester are useless. She will be teaching all new classes.

***

With ten days before the start of school, Sofie sits catatonically staring at blank paper. Trying so hard to write lesson plans for her three preps for the next eighteen weeks, her brain is numb. She cannot think to save her life. Wavy light forms in her peripheral vision. Time for pain meds before a full-fledged migraine. Sofie stumbles to the kitchen for water and Tylenol. Taking two pills out of the bottle, she pops them in her mouth and washes down the little miracle drug with coffee.

Going back to her notebook and text books, Sofie sighs, "That's better. Now, if I'm not prepared, I will not live through my first day back."

Her mind keeps going back to the first days of last semester. How confident she was going into the classroom but, she was totally unprepared. Her classes were disastrous. She keeps focusing on everything that went wrong last semester, until she is paralyzed with panic.

Sofie does everything she can to avoid the lesson planning. It is too painful. She reads, washes clothes, washes dishes three times a day. She cleans her house, gardens, shops, anything not school related. She does all these things and more to keep from thinking about the commitment to teach one more semester in that junior high school in Los Angeles.

With only four days to go before school starts, she does the only thing she can think to do. Sofie calls her best friend, Alex, a physics teacher she met while earning her teaching credential at the university. She hopes Alex can nurse her out of the anxiety attack.

Picking up the phone, Sofie calls Alex.

"Hello?"

"Alex, this is Sofie."

"Sofie?"

"Alex. I need you...desperately."

"What's up, Sofie?"

Alex listens for half an hour to all Sofie's fears. Then he gives her the reassurance she needs. Alex reminds Sofie of all her successes she shared with him, including making the raisins dance. Alex gives Sofie back her confidence she lost while in panic mode. Alex gives her ideas for labs and lesson plans, and reminds her there are always films or videos when she is too tired to teach. Alex helps her laugh again about her first semester failures. Alex helps her see she can make it one more semester, one day at a time.

Starting with baby steps, and three days before school starts, Sofie plots and plans out her destiny for herself and her classes for the next eighteen weeks.

CHAPTER 20

BACK TO SCHOOL

Going back to the classroom, Sofie is reminded of the words of Emma O'Brien, one of the assistant principals, "It does get better...and then it gets worse." Miss O'Brien went on to say, "There will always be good days and bad days. You'll get better at teaching. When the number of good days out number the bad days, you can consider yourself a good teacher."

And Miss O'Brien was right. The first week back Sofie feels her classes are 100 percent better than last semester. She is more organized and more in control. She reorganizes the desks in a horseshoe arrangement, so she can reach all her students. In her teaching credential classes at the university, the theory is that any student more than three rows back, will probably not learn. Sofie's goals are much simpler her second semester. Teach her students good study habits and give them an interest in science and math. If she can accomplish that goal, she will be happy and consider herself successful.

The first week back to school, many of Sofie's former students come by her classroom just to say hello.

"Hi, Ms. Rich." Maria pokes her head into Sofie's classroom door, "Did you miss me?"

"Sure did, Maria," Sofie says with a smile, remembering Maria always tries her best in class. She always participates in the lessons and turns in her homework. Maria is the oldest in her family of seven kids. She never takes a book home, for fear she will lose it or be called a "school girl" and get bullied. But she always copies the assignment and most of the time finishes her work in class or at lunch.

"How was your summer, Ms. Rich?" Delia says, hanging over Maria's shoulder.

"Good! Took a train trip around the U.S. Picked up some samples of stuff for marine biology class," Sofie replies. "How was yours?"

"Good. Worked in my family's restaurant during the busy times." Delia smiles back. "Got a boyfriend now. Met him in the restaurant. He's really cute!"

"You be careful, Delia. You know what they all want at this age. You want to graduate from the ninth, don't you?" Sofie warns.

"I know, I know, Ms. Rich. I'm careful. I'm not givin' myself to him until we're married. My grandmamma already gave me that lecture," Delia tells Sofie.

"Good," Sofie says.

"Hey Ms. Rich. How's it hangin'?" says Big Mike, leaning against the door jam.

"Same as always, Mike," Then remembering Big Mike sitting in the back of the room asleep, Sofie adds, "Are you going to stay awake in my class and do some work?"

"Whatever's clever, Ms. Rich," is Big Mike's standard answer.

"I hope so, Mike, because I am going to call on you, for *sure* today. No more sleeping in the back of the class, hear? I don't want to talk to your parents the first week of school." Sofie threatens.

"Okay, Ms. Rich. Okay," Big Mike agrees.

Many of Sofie's former students are in her current classes. Sofie is delighted so many of them remember her.

By the end of the second week back, teaching starts to get a little rougher. The usual distracting activities start up again. Her eighth-grade boys still love to throw paper airplanes, wads of paper, paper clips and spitballs. The girls in all classes begin their constant chatter in English or Spanish. In fact, they talk so much, they don't even know they are talking. Sofie puts the talking ones right in the very front row. She stands right in front of Ana trying to teach a lesson in science, and Ana *still* talks.

Sofie can no longer stand Ana's constant talking while trying to teach the lesson. Finally, Sofie says, "Ana! Don't talk when I am talking."

"I'm not talking, Ms. Rich."

"Ana, your lips are moving. Words and sounds are coming out of your mouth. That is called talking," Sofie says sarcastically.

"I'm not talking, Ms. Rich," Ana repeats with a little whine in her voice. "Why do you always say I'm talking?"

"Ana, you *are* always talking. You're talking back to me right now, right at this very instant. You need to talk less and listen more. Do you understand?" Sofie's irritation is growing. Ana can tell by the tone of Sofie's voice.

"All right, Ms. Rich! All right! I'll stop talking. Just take a Tic-Tac, okay?" Ana says rudely, suggesting Sofie has bad breath. Ana does not like Sofie getting into her space. She feels singled out. She lashes out with hostility.

Then Camille shouts, "Yuck! What's this?" She reaches up and touches her hair with her hand and is horrified when she feels something sticky. "Ms. Rich," she whines. "I got gum in my hair! Somebody put gum in my hair!"

The boys in the back row turn to one another and start giggling. They are well into their machismo phase: tagging in books, writing on desks, throwing spitballs, shooting paper wads with rubber bands, throwing chalk. Their favorite game is taking apart pens to shoot bits of gum through the barrel. This time Camille's hair is the target. The boys are older now. No longer interested in sailing the paper airplane and into more creative mischief. At the end of the day, Sofie looks at all the stuff on the floor in the front of the room where she stands. One question comes to mind, is she the moving target these junior high school students are trying to hit?

CHAPTER 21

IDENTIFIED FLYING OBJECTS

One of the worst days came on September 27th, less than one month after second semester started. It was a Monday.

Just the Friday before, Sofie sent Julio to the dean's office for throwing fake dog shit around the class. The fake dog shit was made of molded plastic, and looked very real. Julio hit several other students in the back of the head with the vulgar item, causing a major disturbance in Sofie's marine science class.

When Sofie tells Dean Ortega what happened, to her surprise, he corrects her saying, "Feces, fake dog *feces*. Ms. Richmond, we do not use the word *s-h-i-t* in the classroom."

The following Monday, another student in the same marine science class thinks it will be funny to throw something bigger at Sofie, the moving target. For an instant, Sofie makes the mistake of turning her back to the students. In that instant, a pipe from the bottom of a broken chair, a foot long and an inch in diameter, is thrown across the room. It clangs and clatters across the floor, barely missing her as well as several other students.

Stunned, Sofie looks in the direction the pipe came from. There are four possible suspects. Can it be Little Carlitos, only four feet tall, with big brown eyes and the looks of a cherub, dimples set deep in his chubby cheeks? Maybe it is Luis, his behemoth sidekick, as tall as Sofie but twice her weight? Perhaps it is Adolfo, tall and skinny and on probation? Or is it Juan, usually silent, while always eating something in class he brings from the cafeteria where he works?

Sofie asks Maria, a reliable student, "Go get the Dean." Sofie waits, but no one comes. So Sofie walks over and stands behind the possible four, continuing to conduct class until the bell rings. She excuses all but the four boys she suspects and a witness to who saw what happened.

"Okay you guys, Carlitos, Luis, Adolfo, and Juan," Sofie says, "Let's take a little trip down to the Dean's office and tell him which one of you boys threw the pipe at me."

"I saw them throw it," says Gloria, pointing in the direction of the four boys.

"Gloria, will you come along and say what you saw?" Sofie asks the girl.

"Sure, Ms. Rich. It almost hit me too!" replies Gloria, anxious to get even.

"Okay. Let's go," says Sofie to the boys. She leads the little parade of bad boys to the Dean Ortega's office, while the other kids on campus stare and try to find out what crime was committed.

"What have we here, Ms. Richmond?" asks Dean Ortega.

"Well, I was just standing at one end of the classroom having students read from the book, and someone from the other side of the room, throws a foot-long pipe pulled from under a chair. It sailed clean across the room, hitting my desk and chair behind me. They were aiming at me!" Sofie is fuming now, "but it could have hit any one of my students in the front row. Gloria saw it happen. Isn't that true Gloria?" Sofie says, turning to look at Gloria.

"Yes, Ms. Rich, clean 'cross the room! Scared the snot out of me!" Gloria declares, eyes piercing the four boys against the wall of the room.

"I didn't do it! I swear on my mother's honor, I didn't do it!" pleads Adolfo.

"It wasn't me," Juan mutters, breaking his silence while finishing off a bag of chips.

"Carlitos, man, tell them," urges Luis wanting no part of it.

Then they the all start talking feverishly to Carlitos, but in Spanish.

"Quiet!" yells Dean Ortega. Then he picks up the phone and calls for the campus police.

When the campus police arrive, the Dean and police officers pull the boys out in the hall one at a time for questioning. Sofie starts to file charges against Carlitos when he comes back to apologize to her.

Dean Ortega looks at Sofie and says, "If Carlitos apologizes, will you let him back into the classroom?"

"No!" Sofie says angrily.

"Why did you do such a thing, Carlitos?" the Dean asks the small boy.

Carlitos just shrugs. "I don't know. Bored, I guess."

Sofie is so angry, she starts shaking. Looking directly at her student, she shouts, "You could have hurt any one of your classmates. And you tell me, you don't know why you did this?" Her voice now high pitched and strained from her anger.

***

Her thoughts drift back a few days ago to a conversation with Carlitos' English teacher. Sofie remembers asking Mr. Ewing what he knew about Carlitos. His answer was not what Sofie anticipated, "I have tried so hard to get him to do something, anything in my class, besides gang mottos on desks. The kid is illiterate. He cannot read or write English."

Her compassion button hit squarely on the head, she thought, *a lost child in the urban jungle needed a teacher like her to turn him around.*

***

Now, standing in front of the small child, she realizes she is wrong, almost *dead* wrong. She feels that churning in the pit of her stomach again. *No one wants to do anything to little Carlitos, the future serial killer, who does not know why he threw a metal pipe at his teacher. Nor does he see anything wrong with it.* The administration wants Sofie just to forgive and forget, let bygones be bygones. *What's wrong with this picture?* Sofie keeps asking herself.

84

Later in the day, Sofie talks to her mentor teacher, Mr. Jones, about the pipe incident. He tells Sofie it is time to have a little talk with the principal, Mrs. Castillo.

So, after school, Sofie pays a little visit to Mrs. Castillo. Sofie proceeds to tell her about the conduct of certain students who are throwing things. She also tells the principal about the whole pipe incident. Sofie is so angry, her voice blurts out the words, "I will *not* be a frigging moving target in class!"

At that very moment, Mr. Griswold, the assistant principal handling the case walks in. "You realize, Ms. Richmond, you cannot file charges against the child because you did not actually *see* him throw the pipe, even though the child confessed," Mr. Griswold says calmly.

Mrs. Castillo starts calling parents while Sofie sits in her office. She makes a big show of it and assures Sofie Mr. Griswold will come by and talk to the students in her class the next day.

"Well, what about the incident of the fake dog shit?" Sofie asks.

Mr. Griswold flinches a little and then writes *artificial feces* down in his little black notebook.

The next day little Carlitos is gone. He is now an "Opportunity Transfer" better known as OT, to another school in the district. *Now he can harass a whole new set of teachers,* Sofie savors the thought of little Carlitos is someone else's problem.

Word spreads that Carlitos is kicked out of school. Students come around Sofie's classroom, taunting Sofie, "Did you get hit by a pipe, Ms. Rich?"

"No!" is all Sofie says.

In fifth period, eighth-grade marine science, the assistant principal, Mr. Griswold, walks in. Sofie wonders, *when is that fat old man going to say something to my class to put the fear of God in them?* But he says nothing. He just sits down in the back of the classroom and observes Sofie teaching her class.

After class, during Sofie's conference period, Mr. Griswold takes out his little black notebook and proceeds to tear Sofie apart with comments such as, "You know, Ms. Richmond, your seating chart is all wrong. The students are too close together. They need more direction. You should have hand-outs for each unit. Oh, by the way," Mr. Griswold adds, "it is unprofessional to use the word s-h-i-t. The proper or professional term to be used is *feces*."

What is wrong with this picture? Sofie thinks, shaking her head in disbelief. She is no longer the victim of attempted assault with a metal pipe. She is now, according to Mr. Griswold, the one to blame for a student throwing a pipe because the seating chart is wrong, and she did not have hand-outs for her students.

***

Sofie calls in sick the next day, or more correctly, takes a mental health day. After all, she did not want to end up like Mrs. Vierma whom is now a permanent resident at Seaside Sanitarium in a small room on the west side, conveniently padded. When the electro-shock therapy no longer worked, the doctors put her on a heavy dose of lithium. At last, the hallucinations of junior high school kids tormenting her faded, along with most of her long-term memory. Since being heavily medicated, the attendants only occasionally find her in the corner of her room, wide eyed, shrieking out the words, "*SECURITY! SECURITY!*" Mrs. Vierma is finally content in the sheltered environment of Seaside, with far fewer thoughts to trouble her.

That is the day Sofie decides to tough it out until the end of the semester. Then when her contract runs out at the end of January she is running out with it.

CHAPTER 22

THE CURSE OF THE SKULL

On Sofie's mental health day, she goes for therapy to Doctor Pacific, referring to the Pacific Ocean and the beach running alongside it. Sofie always goes to the sea when she feels her sanity slipping in this insane world. There is something about being at the edge of America, looking out at the infinite vastness of the ocean that puts all her infinitesimal problems in perspective. There is something soothing about watching the endless motion of the waves, rhythmically rolling, crashing on the smooth shore, pulling in all the impurities left by man, cleaning the beach of debris. Rocks and shells rolling into the sea, then returning polished along with other treasures.

It is there, Sofie finds her answer. God sends her a sign, a big one. As she walks along the sandy beach, collecting a few choice treasures for her marine science class, the Good Lord washes up a huge object right before her bare feet. It is chalky white in color and as large as a football. *What is it?* She ponders, looking down at the thing that comes to rest right at her feet. *Is it a rock?* She wonders, reaching down to pluck it from the sand before the endless blue-green ocean reclaims it.

To her amazement, it is a skull! The skull is picked clean by the never-ending food chain, smoothed and polished by the constant tumbling of the waves and bleached by the sun. It is in perfectly preserved condition. Sofie can see it was a carnivore, a meat eater, by ten of the fourteen remaining pointed teeth on each side. In front of the mouth, between the pointed, stained teeth, are four small, slightly chisel-ended teeth. Above the small teeth is the nasal cavity. As Sofie looks through the cavity, she can see wavy canals. Behind the nose are deeply hollowed sockets where the eyes of this long-dead creature once resided. The elongated eye sockets to the brain cavity are picked clean. Sofie holds up the skull and looks right through the eye and nose cavities to the other side. At the base of the brain cavity is a socket, where it looks like the spine hooked up to it. But it appears to be positioned horizontally to the skull, instead of vertically like in most mammals. The biggest mystery is the ridge along the top of the skull. From between the eye sockets to the back of the brain cavity, a strange ridge of bone stands up an inch high like a bony fin. The cold, salty seawater drifts around Sofie's ankles as she studies the skull of the unknown creature.

At first glance, it appears to be a dog's head. But if it is a dog's skull, how did it get into the ocean? Sofie announces to the Pacific Ocean, "What a great lesson plan for marine science! Thank you, God! I'll tell my classes if they misbehave, I'll put 'The Curse of The Skull' upon them. Then I'll allow the students to observe the skull as scientists, describing what they observe, conclude with an educated guess what kind of animal once owned this skull. Finally, theorize what happened to the skull's owner and describe how the skull found its way to the beach."

Sofie gazes off into the distant horizon, that crisp hazy October morning and says to the world, "It's almost Halloween. Perfect timing! I'm ready now to go back into the trenches with new weapons: curiosity and wonder. Something to make them think of something other than destruction and distraction. Something to put the fear of God in them!"

***

The next morning, bright and early, before any of her students come to class, Sofie writes on the board in big bold letters:

**THE CURSE OF THE SKULL WILL BE UPON
ALL THOSE WHO MISBEHAVE!
WHAT IS IT?
WHERE DID IT COME FROM??
HOW DID IT GET THERE???**

The students come in, sit down, and read the board, then start whispering to one another. That's when Sofie brings out the skull and reads the first line out loud. "The Curse of The Skull will be upon all those who misbehave!"

A dead silence falls over the classroom, then a burst of chatter. Sofie walks down each aisle with the skull in hand so all the students can get a good look at it. To those particularly mischievous boys, Sofie gives a little lunge of the skull toward them, causing them to jump back in surprise.

"What is it?" they all ask.

"What is it?" Sofie asks them in turn. "Look at the teeth. What does it eat? What is it?" Sofie asks again.

"It's a dog, Ms. Rich! It's a dog!" Some are saying.

"Is it?" Sofie questions. "Look at the nose. You can see right through. Look at where the eye sockets are. Are those eye and nose cavities of a dog?" Sofie teases.

"It's a dog! Trust me, it's a dog!" Big Mike shouts out.

"It eats meat; it's a meat-eater!" Maria says, analyzing the pointy teeth.

"It's a carnivore! It's a dog!" Billy yells, jumping out of his seat.

All the students are talking at once.

"Is it a dog?" Sofie asks again. "Look closely at where the spine would be. It comes straight out. Look inside the skull, where the brain was. It's been picked clean, by what?" Sofie asks the marine science class.

"Sharks!"

"Crabs!"

"Those little bugs in the water. Plankton! That's it, Plankton!"

They are all shouting with excitement. Sofie smiles at the students all trying to solve the mystery of the skull.

"It's a dog. Trust me, Ms. Rich. It's a dog!" one of her baggy-pants students insists.

"Do you think a dog has a one-inch bony ridge along the top of his skull?" Sofie says, watching the reaction of the class.

Curiosity grips the students and Maria speaks up and asks, "Where did you get it, Ms. Rich? Did you kill it and eat it?"

"No, of course not. I found the skull on the beach. The waves tossed it out of the ocean, right in front of me. A gift from God placed at my feet."

"If it *is* a dog," Sofie pauses to pique their curiosity, "how did it get into the ocean, and wash up on the beach? What do you think happened to the dog if, indeed, it is a dog's head? You are all marine scientists. Describe what you see. Tell me what you think it is, what happened to it, and how it got here. This is your assignment for today."

As if by magic, all Sofie's students, even the bad boys, whip out paper and pencil. Feverishly, they all start writing at break-neck speed, until the bell rings. As they leave the room, some students ask Sofie if she knows what it is.

"Honestly, I don't know. But I'll find out," Sofie says.

A few students guess correctly. It is a sea lion's skull, a male sea lion or elephant seal, to be exact. Whatever it is, The Curse of The Skull brings Sofie new-found respect, even among her worst and most troublesome students. She is once again in control, thanks to the skull.

CHAPTER 23

OPENING WORMS

I n control again of her marine science class, Sofie feels she can safely move into dissections. After all, dissections are performed using sharp objects, such as scalpels. At John Quincy Junior High, in the heart of gangland territory, scalpels are considered lethal weapons outside the classroom. Following directions and procedures when handling lab equipment is of the utmost importance.

Sofie decides to talk to the dissection expert on campus, Dr. Koil, who has a PhD in medicine and teaches Biology at John Quincy. Dr. Koil is a strange combination of man and beast, a tall, thin, pale, middle-aged man, his jet-black hair slicked back to collar length. A white lab coat usually covers his street clothes, generally a dark shirt and slacks. He studied to be a medical doctor, but after years of schooling and degrees, he declined to take his internship, leaving him with the title of Doctor, but not the profession.

Needing money, as we all do, he changed professions and is now the life science teacher at John Quincy Junior High School. He has a real love for reptiles and a collection that rivals any zoo. Along with various boa and other snakes, he owns several two-foot-long iguanas, and a five-foot-long alligator he named Elvis.

It is Dr. Koil whom Sofie consulted on the skull. It seems only proper to consult him on dissections. After all, he is a doctor as well as a science teacher and of all the teachers on campus, probably the ultimate authority on dissections.

Sofie is right. Dr. Koil instructs her on everything she needs to know about dissecting biological specimens in class and more. Dr. Koil is also a chain-talker and once he starts talking, will talk non-stop for at least thirty minutes, unless interrupted by the tardy bell.

Dr. Koil keeps his biology students in line by arranging all the cages of snakes and rats lining the perimeter of his classroom. The ultimate heavy is, of course, Elvis, the alligator. Elvis lives in a large cage in his supply room in a swampy environment made especially for Elvis. Students take turns feeding Elvis once a day. Occasionally, Dr. Koil brings Elvis out on a leash and a very strong chain with a leather muzzle strapped around his powerful jaws.

When Sofie comes to ask for advice on dissection of worms, Dr. Koil is preoccupied with building a tropical rain forest for his reptiles outside his classroom. He is never too busy to talk science. Dr. Koil takes thirty minutes out of his schedule to tell Sofie his secret to success on classroom dissections.

"You see, Ms. Richmond," Dr. Koil, in his infinite wisdom, begins, "I break my class up into surgical teams of four. We have a surgeon, who cuts, an assistant surgeon, who helps the surgeon and examines. Then we have a nurse, who handles the instruments and assists the surgeons. And the fourth member of the team is the anesthesiologist, who writes everything down and draws the specimen. There is something for everyone. That way those who want to cut do, and those who don't want to cut don't have to. Everyone is involved, and everyone is happy. It's as simple as that."

***

True to his word, dissection was as simple as Dr. Koil said it would be. Sofie writes on the board the procedures for dissections and the team players just as Dr. Koil defined them:

Surgeon–one who cuts

Assistant Surgeon–one who helps the surgeon and examines

Nurse–one who handles the instruments and assists the surgeons

Anesthesiologist–one who writes down procedures and draws the specimen.

"Do we get to cut open worms, Ms. Rich?" Molly asks. Her vocabulary, as well as the rest of the LEP students in the class, did not include the word *dissect* meaning to cut apart, to separate into pieces, to expose the several parts for scientific examination, to analyze and interpret minutely.

"Huh, do we? Do we get to open worms today?" Molly repeats.

"No." Sofie replies, trying to sound like a true scientist. "We will *dissect* worms today." Then she introduces the word *dissection* and explains the procedures. All the students cheer.

Busily, they form into their Surgical Teams. Everyone is happy as Dr. Koil predicted.

"Do you want to cut?" Jose asks, turning to Jamie.

"Yeah, I want to cut. I want to be a surgeon," Jamie tells Jose.

"All right! I want to cut, too. Let me be your assistant surgeon and we can both be on the same team!" Jose responds eagerly. "Who are we going to get for our Nurse?"

"Yuck!" Melissa moans. "I don't want to touch those slimy things. I want to be the anesthe...or whatever that word is, that doesn't have to cut."

"Anesthesiologist," Sofie injects.

"Whatever," Melissa moans again, "Just as long as I don't have to touch those smelly worms."

"Can I be a nurse?" Maria begs Jose and Jamie. I want to be the nurse and get all the stuff together to operate. Like they did on my nana, when they took her gallbladder out."

"Sure, Maria, we can always use a pretty nurse," Jose says laughingly, as she joins their team.

Soon everyone is part of a surgical team, sitting excitedly together at their own operating table. Sofie brings out the bucket of worms! Everyone cheers. She brings out the dissection trays. Carefully, she brings out the scalpels, picks, pins, and the tweezers. The pungent smell of formaldehyde fills the air.

Worms are being opened and examined by wide-eyed junior scientists, fascinated by the insides of these long, slimy creatures. Totally engrossed by the procedures and results, they are all serious students, intent to do the best dissection ever performed by a surgical team. They call Sofie over to their operating tables to examine their handiwork.

"Can you locate the sex organs, to determine whether the worm was a boy or a girl?" Sofie asks. Anxiously, they look and poke about, until they find the sex of the worm.

"It's a girl!" Manual shouts excitedly.

They are learning, Sofie thinks to herself. *They are learning new things from me, these Limited English Proficiency students.* She feels the warm glow of achievement come over her. She is a teacher, at last, and a good one at that!

***

The long drive back home that night flies by as Sofie recalls the day's dissection labs, and the faces of each member of the surgical teams that perform dissections.

There is only one nagging question in her mind that night. She is one scalpel short. Did one of her students steal a scalpel? That dissecting instrument could be considered a deadly weapon outside of the classroom. Or did she simply miscount the equipment? Next time she must tighten the control on the distribution and collection of dissecting equipment.

CHAPTER 24

OT KIDS

There are only five black students in a sea of Hispanic faces at Sofie's school. The few blacks in Sofie's classes are mostly Opportunity Transfers, better known as OTs. Which means this handful of students did something so awful at their old school, they were kicked out and sent to another school. Like little Carlitos, the Latino cutie with the dimples, who threw the pipe at Sofie, he became an OT to another school in the district.

Of the five black OTs, there is Nathan, four feet, two inches in height with a deep set of dimples in his chocolate brown face. He never stops talking and moves constantly from chair to chair. He is smart when he applies himself and can finish all assignments way ahead of the rest of the class. However, he is seldom motivated to do so. He manages to earn good grades with very little effort. However, Nathan is very sneaky, priding himself on what he can get away with.

Then there is Nathan's sidekick, Walker. Walker is a big easy-going guy, but not too bright. Walker does anything his friend, Nathan, asks him to do. Why? Nathan has all the answers, that's why. Nathan slips Walker the answers to the tests and does Walker's homework. That is precisely why Nathan is so smart, he does the homework for all his friends, so they will like him.

Then there is Joey. Skinny, wiry Joey is another constant talker and mover. He knows nothing, because he is always sent out of the classroom to detention for behavior. He is never in class long enough to learn anything. Learning is painful for him. When he cannot get the answers from his friend, Nathan, Joey's usual comment is, "I hate this class."

Sofie tries to help Joey with his classroom assignments in math, but whenever she gets too close, Joey says, "I hate math." then fanning the air in front of his face with his hand, says, "Pooh, man, I think you need a Tic-Tac." If Sofie insists he read or work on the assignment in class, he starts sucking his thumb and with the other hand, fondles his ear. He then pulls his knees up into a fetal position and stares at Sofie with daggers.

Then there is Noah, who transferred in from Belize, Central America. Noah is bigger than Walker, probably five feet eight. His hair is twisted into dread-locks and he wears the baggy pants of a tagger. Baggy pants are known to hide anything from knives and guns to marking pens and spray paint cans. Noah talks slowly and always needs a lot of help. Noah waits until Sofie explains the assignment to the entire class, and then asks for individual help. Noah writes even slower than he talks. He remedies his inability to under-stand class assignments by cutting class. Within a few weeks, the school administration OTs Noah out to another unsuspecting school.

Last, but by no means the least is Deshawn. At thirteen years of age, Deshawn is already six feet tall and obviously still growing. He towers over all the other students in Sofie's classes. When he transfers into Sofie's science class, she does not know John Quincy Junior High is Deshawn's fourth school. Sofie doesn't know Deshawn's father is in jail for murder. All she sees is a tall lanky kid, with "Buckwheat" hair and a big smile saying, "I'm going to do all my work in this class, Ms. Rich. I'm going to get an A in your class." At first it is true, but as he interacts with the other four black OT students, trouble begins.

Soon Deshawn is working harder on his social skills than his science lessons. He is talking to anyone sitting next to him more and more often. Sofie tries moving him to different classroom locations, searching to find a seat in her room where he will focus on his class work and not talk. Sofie tries standing over Deshawn to discourage him from talking and encourage him to do his assignments. A change comes over Deshawn. He no longer tries to do his best work. Indeed, he does no classwork at all. He becomes paranoid about Sofie's closeness, her scrutinizing his lack of class participation. Deshawn moves to the back of the class with the other four black students for a group project. That's when the gum wads start flying from the back, landing in the hair of several students. Sofie cannot tell exactly who the culprit is, so she sends the whole back row out to detention.

Deshawn protests, claiming his innocence. Lashing out at Sofie, he threatens to slash her tires. "Better check your tires before you drive home, Ms. Rich."

Sofie tries not to let Deshawn's remark bother her, but she is out of there at the three o'clock bell.

It was several weeks after that encounter with Deshawn that the real threat comes. Sofie feels the need to have a lab in the physical science class Deshawn is enrolled in, hoping to increase his interest.

She plans a lab locating epicenters of earthquakes. To do so requires the use of a compass, an instrument used to draw circles. At one end of the instrument is a small pencil, at the other end a two-inch metal spike. Sofie remembers her uneasiness over the possible missing scalpel a few weeks ago.

In the classroom she instructs her aide, "Be sure to count and monitor the compasses. I don't want to lose any sharply pointed objects."

"You got it, Ms. Richmond. Don't worry. I'll be sure to pick them all up at the end of the class," Sofie's aide, Mike says. He hands out thirty compasses and all thirty students are busy following the instructions on the board to plot epicenters. Everyone is in their seats drawing circles around points on a map. Success.

The time comes to clean up, and Mike goes to each desk to collect the compasses. One is missing. Only twenty-nine are turned in. An instrument with a two-inch metal point can be considered a weapon. Sofie feels uneasy about the missing compass. She scans the classroom, looking for signs of someone hiding something.

"Okay class, one of the compasses is missing. Please turn it in now." Sofie tells the class. "No one leaves for lunch until the missing lab equipment, the compass for drawing circles, is returned."

"Are you sure you counted right, Ms. Rich?" Yolanda whines, "I don't wanna miss lunch with my friends because someone's stupid enough to keep that stupid thing."

"I don't have it. I wanna to go," yells out Joey, ready to dash out the door.

"I turned mine in," shouts Nathan, showing his anger by spitting on the floor.

"Let us go, Ms. Rich, Let us go!" They are all talking at once again.

"Well students, I'm sorry. I guess we'll have to search backpacks," Sofie says in a sad voice. "I don't like holding all of you from lunch, but I *have* to have all the school equipment and instruments back." Then turning to her classroom aide, she says, "Mike, you start at the front and I'll start at the back."

Mike starts shuffling through backpacks, "Okay, Melissa, you're clear. Jaime, you're clean. Deshawn, what's this?" Mike reaches into Deshawn's shirt pocket to discover the missing pointy instrument, possible weapon.

"Everyone can go to lunch now, except Deshawn, that is," Sofie announces to the class. Then turning to Deshawn, she says, "Come over here, Deshawn, I'm going to write you up for three hours of detention for stealing."

Anger wells up in the tall teenager. "Don't you touch me!" Deshawn lashes out. "Don't touch me or I'll put a fist through your face." he threatens.

"Now you've done it, Deshawn," Mike warns. "Now you're in big trouble."

Sofie clings to her cool as best she can. Calmly, without emotion says, "Come over here, Deshawn. I'm writing you up for five hours of detention now, for stealing and making threats." Sofie takes a deep breath, and slowly lets the air out of her lungs. She tries to remain calm and keep from shaking. She fears any sign of her emotional state, may result in retaliation from the angry black student, prone to violence.

"You really did it *now*, Deshawn, you really done it this time. Man, you're in really big trouble now." Mike keeps warning Deshawn, while Sofie presses her pen hard on the paper, writing down exactly what happened and what was said. She feels a flush of anguish, wondering why she ever left a safe profession like accounting.

"There. Done. Now Mike, escort Deshawn to the Dean's office and take this referral with you," Sofie says, handing Mike the referral form.

"Okay, Ms. Richmond," Mike says. Turning to Deshawn, says, "Come on, Deshawn, you have a date with Dean Ortega." Mike puts his hand on Deshawn's shoulder. Angrily, Deshawn shakes it off and turns to Sofie, glaring at her with hate in his eyes.

Sofie thinks that is the end of it, but it is only the beginning of a new set of problems. Mike takes Deshawn away, while a crowd of students gather at the open door to witness all the drama.

Sofie closes the door after Mike leaves with Deshawn and does her best to collect her thoughts. She reaches for her red thermos bottle and unscrews the plastic cap. Pouring some hot coffee into her cup, she spills a bit over the rim and onto a blank referral slip. She sighs and takes a sip of the golden-brown liquid, wondering what will happen to Deshawn.

Just as Sofie is calming her nerves, there's a knock on the door. Mike bursts in, rapidly spilling out the news of what occurred in the assistant principal's office.

"Ms. Richmond, Mr. Griswold wants to revoke Deshawn's OT and send him back to his original school," he says breathlessly.

"Good," Sofie replies emotionless. She is completely drained, and the coffee is not helping.

"But that's not all," Mike says, his eyes widening in fear for Ms. Richmond. "When the assistant principal told Deshawn he is sending him back, Deshawn went and told him a lie. He said you grabbed him and called him S-H-I-T. So now, Mr. Griswold, is planning to pull you into a parent-teacher conference about what happened."

With the media's focus on the Rodney King beatings, Sofie is no longer the victim again, but the one to blame. She leaves school that Thursday afternoon as soon as the three o'clock bell rings. She needs to update her grade book and get ready for a conference.

Sofie racks her brain recalling the last three weeks. "Has Deshawn done any work lately? No. I need proof. I need to make sure all the assignments are recorded."

Friday, Deshawn is not in class. Suspended.

Monday comes. Toward the end of Sofie's first period class, a heavy-set black woman, opens the door at the back of the classroom. All the students turn to look at the lady motioning to Sofie to come to the door. It is the dreaded Mrs. Malcolm, the other Dean of Discipline, who comes like the angel of death, when things are so bad they can't get any worse. The room is dead silent, students wondering what horrible thing happened and what is about to happen to their teacher.

Sofie walks up to Mrs. Malcolm, ready for the battle she knows will come.

"Ms. Richmond, would you step outside with me please." The words coming out of the woman's mouth sound as smooth and sweet as black molasses. But Sofie knows the words to come will not be so sweet. They are deadly serious and can be the death of her teaching career. "I have Deshawn, his mother, Mrs. Riley, and Mr. Griswold outside. We'd like to speak to you about the incident last Thursday."

Sofie looks passed Mrs. Malcolm to see Mr. Griswold talking with Deshawn and his mother. A chill runs down Sofie's spine, causing her to throw her shoulders back and stand up straight as she possibly can. Four to one, the odds are against her.

Mrs. Malcolm continues, "Mr. Griswold wants to have a little conference with you, about Deshawn. I'll take over your class." Now all eyes turn from Mrs. Malcolm to Sofie. The room full of junior high students start to whisper to one another.

"Quiet class, and turn around," booms Mrs. Malcolm. "Get back to your assignment!" With that, silence falls over the classroom again like a heavy wet blanket. Students quickly turn around and open their books, pretending to read, glancing at one another. They know this may be the end of Ms. Richmond.

"Just a minute," Sofie says, looking outside again. She sees Mr. Griswold, nodding to whatever Deshawn and his mother are saying. All are black and at least a head taller than Sofie. She knows this will be a battle. She needs ammunition.

"Just let me grab my grade book," Sofie says fearlessly to Mrs. Malcolm, even though she is shaking inside like jelly.

CHAPTER 25

THE SHOWDOWN

With her grade book in hand, Mr. Griswold leads Sofie into a vacant room. There sits Deshawn and his tall black mother, Mrs. Riley. The first thing Sofie notices, Deshawn's long wooly hair is gone, shaven clean off. He looks like a totally different person. No longer does he look defiant, but just a meek oversized kid.

"Good morning, Deshawn. Nice haircut," Sofie acknowledges the new look. Deshawn just nods but says not a word.

"This is Deshawn's mother, Mrs. Riley," Mr. Griswold says, introducing Sofie to the student's mother. "Please, sit down Ms. Richmond."

"This is about what happened last week..." Mr. Griswold begins.

Sofie feels the knot in her stomach tightening as she pulls out the roll book where she records all assignments the students complete. "Mrs. Riley," she interrupts Mr. Griswold in mid sentence to address Deshawn's mother. "I am so glad to meet you. Deshawn hasn't done any work for the past two weeks, and the last grade was a D minus." Sofie opens her roll book to show Deshawn's mother his grades. "I don't know what is going on," Sofie continues. "Deshawn started out really good, but now he is in danger of failing my class. I have tried everything to get Deshawn to do his classwork. I have moved him to different seats away from his friends, but he still talks with anyone sitting next to him. He does not stay in his seat, and because he is constantly talking, he does not hear the assignment or how to do it. Then, he asks me to explain everything all over again, individually to him. When I look over his shoulder to see what he's doing, or if he needs help, he gets

101

defensive. I want Deshawn to succeed in my class, to learn science and pass, but I can do just so much. I hate to send him out for detention when he talks, because he misses even more and gets farther behind. I just don't know what to do with him," Sofie pleads. Now the focus is on Deshawn.

"Deshawn! This is the *last* time I'm coming to school for you," Deshawn's mother fires at him. Deshawn sits sheepishly silent while his mother continues to rag on him. "There you go again, getting in with the wrong crowd. Deshawn, I like this school. This is a good school. I have two little ones at home. I don't have the *time* to come down here for you anymore. This is your last chance, Deshawn. I have *had* it with you."

"Well, uh, what about her grabbing me?" Deshawn says, trying to change the focus back to Sofie.

That's when Sofie goes over the series of events leading up to the compass incident. She finishes with, "had Deshawn taken the compass out of the classroom, it's a lethal weapon, with far graver consequences. I am protecting Deshawn as well as others."

Then to Sofie's surprise, Mr. Griswold backs her up with, "Ms. Richmond has the right to detain you, Deshawn, by force, if necessary. A teacher is considered the legal parent while the child is in school."

"Well, uh, uh, what about her calling me s-h-i-t." Deshawn still trying to change the focus. He thought he had Sofie now.

Turning to his mother, Sofie confesses, "I'd moved Deshawn up to the front row, next to a very quiet, good student, Rodney. My hope was Deshawn would do his work. I was so frustrated. He still didn't work on his assignment like the rest of his classmates. Instead, he was talking to Rodney, preventing his classmate from doing the assignment. In desperation, I said to Deshawn as quietly as I could, 'Deshawn, you have not *done* s-h-i-t.' I spelled out his *activity*, not calling *him* s-h-i-t. That was it. I apologize if there was any misunderstanding."

To Sofie's astonishment, Mr. Griswold backs her up. "Deshawn, Ms. Richmond is only human." Then to Sofie he asks, "What do you say about giving Deshawn another chance, Ms. Richmond? For only two weeks, Ms. Richmond?"

"Well, I don't know." Sofie hesitates. "It's really up to Deshawn. If he doesn't want to learn in my class, there is no way I can make him learn. I can seat him in a corner by himself, I can explain everything to him individually, I can even write the assignments for him. But if he does not want to learn in my class, or do the work, there is no way he will pass the class."

"What do you say, Deshawn?" Mr. Griswold pleads, rubbing his forehead where his hair used to be with the palm of his hand. "Do you want to stay in Ms. Richmond's class and do the work?"

"Well, uh? Yeah. I guess," Deshawn mumbles. He smooths his hand over the stubby hair roots where a full curly afro once was. He seems to like the feel of course stubble on his head. There is a certain freedom of wash and go hair. So much cooler than the thick course hair he just sheared off. A summer breeze slid through an open window, cooling the room inside.

"Well, Deshawn," Sofie says with a sigh of relief, sucking in the cool air, "we have four more weeks of school left. Let's see if we can make it through. Okay?"

"Okay, Ms. Rich," Deshawn says with a big smile, exposing his dimples. And with that said, Deshawn shakes Sofie's hand and strikes a deal.

"Thank you so much, Mrs. Riley, for taking the time to come down here for Deshawn," Sofie smiles, nodding to Deshawn's mother. "And thank you too, Mr. Griswold, for helping us sort out this problem."

That is the turning point for Deshawn. He returns to class to do his work and Sofie agrees to give him some space. She tells her aide, Mike, to do the same.

At the end of the two weeks, Deshawn comes up to Sofie's desk after class and asks, "What's my grade, Ms. Rich, what's my grade now? I've been doing all my work." Nervously, he bites his lip, hoping for a C to keep him from going back to juvenile prison or probation.

Sofie doesn't know why Deshawn was once incarcerated. However, by his previous reactions when she got too close to him, she thinks it had to do with violence.

"Well Deshawn," Sofie says, looking up from grading papers, into his sad brown eyes, "let's look in the old grade book." Sofie opens the drawer where she keeps her grade book. Its corners are frayed, and pages worn. She flips to period five, runs her finger down the row until she comes to Deshawn Riley. She calculates the average on a small pocket calculator, by adding all the grades and dividing by the number of assignments. Raising her eyebrows, she looks up at Deshawn's face again and says, "Looks like you've brought your D- grade up to a D+."

"Ah, Ms. Rich, I need a C to keep me out of trouble. If I don't get at least a C, they gonna throw me back in the slammer. My mama's gonna be so mad, I'm gonna get another whoopin'," Deshawn pleads, his brown eyes welling up with tears. He wipes the wetness away with his shirt sleeve. "I've been doing all my work, Ms. Rich. What else can I do to get a C? I need a C in your class."

"Well Deshawn, are you willing to do a report for extra credit?" Sofie asks feeling that knot in her stomach tightening again. She wonders what this child could have done to deserve jail time.

"Yes, Ms. Rich. Extra credit. Anything to get a C," Deshawn says, his face lighting up with new hope, his big smile the proof.

"Okay then, choose one of these four astronomers," Sofie says, opening the Physical Science text book. "Research everything about the astronomer you choose and write a ten-page report. I want a rough draft by Tuesday. The final report will have a cover page, at least one drawing, and a bibliography. It must be neatly typed or handwritten in black ink. Do you think you can do that Deshawn, to bring your grade up to a C?"

"Yes, Ms. Rich. Absolutely. I'll do it. You'll see, Ms. Rich," Deshawn says, excitedly. Then second thoughts creep into Deshawn's head. "Ten pages, that's a lot. Does it have to be ten pages?"

"Ten. Is it a deal?" Sofie sticks to her guns.

"Ten pages then, on Galileo. It's a deal." And they shake on it.

Deshawn is true to his word. He brings Sofie the rough draft on Tuesday as promised. She looks it over, makes some suggestions. The following Wednesday, before the end of the semester, Deshawn brings Sofie the final report, ten pages, handwritten in black ink, with two pictures and a bibliography.

Sofie is so pleased, she feels a warm glow in her heart as Deshawn hands her the completed report. She can tell, Deshawn is pleased with his hard work by the smile in his deep brown eyes. "Here, Ms. Rich. Done. Just like I told you I would," he says, handing Sofie his masterpiece.

"Not just done, Deshawn, but well done," Sofie adds with a nod. The report is an A paper.

"Deshawn, this report will definitely bring your grade in the class up to a C-. But I'm going to drop the minus, and give you a straight C," Sofie tells Deshawn, after recalculating his grade.

"Thank you, Ms. Rich. Thank you. Ms. Rich, I want you to know, you are my favorite teacher," Deshawn says with a big toothy grin.

Two days later, Deshawn's mother and his grandma stop by Sofie's room to ask about of his progress. This time Sofie has good news for them.

Yes, Sofie ponders, *I did make a difference with this one...kept him from slipping through the cracks...this time.*

CHAPTER 26

HALLOWEEN DOOR PRIZE

The holidays always bring out the best and the worst in people. Strangely enough, Halloween brought out the best in the worst homeroom ever imagined. Sofie's homeroom from hell is big on sailing paper airplanes in the classroom when Sofie is not looking. This is the homeroom of creative "Kick Me Please" signs to be stuck on the backs of unsuspecting students. This is the homeroom of frequent fights, tagging on desks, constant talking and moving around. This is the homeroom that never listens to the bulletins and Sofie strong-armed into the Flag Salute. This is the homeroom that eventually worked together to win the coveted ice cream party prize for the Scariest Halloween Door Contest.

Starting out with spider webs and skeletons, slowly, the Halloween Door evolved. The skeletons transform to fiends with three heads or four legs. The girl in charge of the organizing brought a hideous mask, a pair of jeans, and red high-top sneakers, creating a monster. Students borrow a boy's jacket, and stuff the mask, jeans, jacket, including the high tops with paper. Slowly, the devil monster begins to take shape. Setting him in a desk chair outside against the opened door, the students drape him with spider webs and rubber or plastic spiders. On the desk in front of the devil monster is the book, *Interstellar Pig* with a monster on the book cover. On the door is a tombstone. It reads:

R.I.P.
Ms. Rich
1901 – 1993

Even the ESL girls who cannot speak English help. The new OT student, Jamie, who is one of ten children, helps decorate. He has a step-father who beats him, and one day carried a gun to school in his poncho pocket. The officer at the school said, "Drop it!" and the gun went off and shot someone in the head. That's when his school sent him over to John Quincy as an OT. Yes, even Jamie helps decorate the door for Halloween.

There is such a fever of excitement. The door décor becomes more and more bizarre. Students from other homerooms come by, ditching their own homerooms, just to see the hideous sight. Sofie's proud of her homeroom's creative students. Large crowds gather at nutrition and lunch. The crowds are so large, that Sofie's homeroom students take turns standing guard until the final judging day.

It is a red-letter day, when Sofie's students hear over the intercom their homeroom wins the Halloween Door contest. They all cheer their shared victory.

The following Tuesday morning during homeroom, the whole class marches triumphantly to the cafeteria to enjoy their prize. They are rewarded with every combination of strawberry, vanilla, and chocolate ice cream and as many toppings as they want. Nuts, caramel and hot fudge sauces are lavishly heaped on mountains of ice cream. Sofie's award winning homeroom students happily devour the sweet treat melting in their mouths. As they kick back, basking in the glow of their fame, they savor the prize for the Scariest Halloween door. All are chatting about their amazingly weird creation, and how they beat every other homeroom.

It is the first and last time Sofie's homeroom students are cohesive. She cherishes the golden memory of this unlikely mix of students, working together on a common goal and winning.

CHAPTER 27

A THANKSGIVING VISIT

Just as Halloween brought out the best in Sofie's homeroom class, strangely enough, Thanksgiving, the day to give thanks, brought out the worst. Returning from four days off over the holiday, Sofie approaches her room bright and early, ready to bring new ideas into the last remaining weeks of the school semester.

Placing the key in the lock, Sofie turns it and opens the door. Her heart sinks to an all-time low. Looking inside her room, she sees someone must have broken into her room during the four-day Thanksgiving holiday. The classroom is totally trashed.

All the walls and chalk boards are tagged in gang writing, done with wide black markers in huge letters. Desktops are marked in the same tagging style. Strangely enough, the NASA space posters of the planets and spacecraft are not tagged. Cabinets are broken into. Papers and referral forms are scattered all over the floor. Chairs are overturned. Total chaos.

Upon looking closer, Sofie notices one of the six microscopes she keeps on the large round table is missing. If students finish their work early, their reward is to look at objects under the microscope. Now one is missing.

Looking closer still, Sofie examines the tagging. High on the wall, above the green chalk boards is something written in English. *YOU'LL NEVER CATCH ME, PIGS.* Then Sofie sees something that makes her want to cry. There on the chalk board, drawn with a wide black marker, a small crown.

She has seen Jose Martinez draw a similar crown on his desk in her math and science classes when he is bored.

Was one of her own students, Jose, the one who trashed her room? She works so hard to reach these youths, to get them interested and involved. Is this the reward for all her hard work and sleepless nights, one of her own student's breaks in and trashes her room? Hot tears well up in Sofie's eyes as she fights back the urge to cry.

She closes her room, not touching anything and looks for the campus police or the assistant principal in charge. Locating Mr. Griswold, Sofie relates what she discovered, including the missing microscope and the drawing of the crown.

"Yes, we know, Ms. Richmond," Mr. Griswold says calmly. "You didn't touch anything, did you?"

"No. Nothing," Sofie replies.

"Good. The campus police will be there soon. They will want to talk with you. Tell them everything for the report," he says. "Don't worry Ms. Richmond. We'll get you another room to teach in. Don't let any students in the room. We'll get it all cleaned up for you. Had you locked the door and cabinets before the Thanksgiving holiday, Ms. Richmond?"

"Of course," Sofie snaps, feeling anger welling up inside. *Of course, I lock the them, I always lock the door and cabinets before I leave for the day.* She hates how Mr. Griswold talks to her as if she is one of the students.

"No need to get excited, Ms. Richmond," Griswold snaps back, then adds in sarcastic tones, "You know, Ms. Richmond, you really should have put away those microscopes." Griswold is referring to the microscopes left on the round table in the back of the room. Sofie always left them out on the round table. Now one is missing after the tagging raid over the Thanksgiving weekend.

Mr. Griswold leads Sofie to an empty bungalow, room seventeen. She is to keep on teaching as if nothing happened. All the while, students from all over the school are trying to get a glimpse inside Sofie's trashed classroom. The broken window, which had only a Plexiglas replacement since the beginning of the school year, was simply pushed in to break into the classroom.

The window was faulty to begin with. It did not take a genius to figure that one out.

Sofie wants to say, "You know Mr. Griswold, you really should have replaced that window with real glass instead of Plexiglas. Maybe it would have prevented the break-in." But she does not say a word. She holds her anger back, and bites her lip to prevent her from saying something she will regret.

"Here's your new room, Ms. Richmond. You can teach your classes here for the day. When the investigation is over, we'll have the janitor clean up your room. It should be done by this evening. We will direct your students to report here," Mr. Griswold says with a smile, as if this is a routine occurrence.

After Griswold leaves, the students come by Sofie's classroom taunting, her saying, "Did they redecorate your room, Ms. Rich?"

"No!" Sofie answers, trying not to show her anger, holding back tears that want to flow. She can cry when she gets home. Never show weakness. Kids in gangs are like dogs. They can sense fear and attack without mercy.

"Do they know who did it, Ms Rich?" Jesse asks, as he fidgets with the pen behind his ear. He is a tagger, too. His crew was not in on this job, but he did not want anyone ratting on him. Anyone caught and convicted of defacing public property means jail time.

"Yes. They know." That is all Sofie says on the matter. Then she drops the subject. She does not want to give out any more information. That is not her job. Her job is to teach. To teach math and science is what she has been hired and paid to do. She does not want any retaliation from any of these kids who are in gangs. You never know what they may do, given a chance. She feels violated, that some kid can break into her classroom and destroy it. Who knows what these kids will do if provoked. She feels like the victim. Is this what Mrs. Vierma, the teacher she replaced, went through just one year ago, before she suddenly disappeared?

Just as Sofie replies to Jesse, she glances over to see the campus police, escorting Jose into her trashed classroom for interrogation. Sofie gasps a breath of air on that cold chilly day, knowing Jose was the one she identified as drawing the crown. With a sigh, she turns into her temporary room, closes the door and starts conducting her homeroom class. The kids are restless, all whispering about the trashed room and the police investigation. Sofie looks down at her seating chart to take roll, trying to concentrate on who is here and who is not?

Suddenly there is a knock at the door. Sofie looks up from her roll book, and all whispers stop. Dead silence envelopes the room. Sofie clears her throat and walks over to the door, opening it. It is the campus police. They enter the room and speak to Sofie in low muffled tones. The students strain to hear what is being said.

"Ms. Richmond, we need to talk to Frank Mendoza," one officer says to Sofie.

Sofie's heart feels heavy and her mind races. Her thoughts spin around in her head. *On no. They want Frank for questioning on the vandalism? Not Frank! Oh please, not Frank. Frank is one of my better students, trying to behave and showing interest in my science class. Not Frank, please don't let it be Frank, dear God,* she prays.

Soon Frank is gone, leaving the classroom with one officer on each side. Frank just shrugs his shoulders, as if he does not care. The two boys, Frank Mendoza and Jose Martinez, are questioned for hours.

By the end of the day, the two boys are released. Jose Martinez, the crown maker, comes by Sofie's classroom in the bungalow. Laughing, he says to her, "Ha ha, it wasn't me."

The next day one of the campus police comes by Sofie's classroom to inform her that Jose told them who taught him how to draw the crown. It was that kid and his brother who did the damage. The police arrest the tagger brothers and promise Sofie they will get back the stolen microscope. It seems, one of the boys tried to pawn the microscope, but the pawnbroker would not accept it. It had L.A.S.D. engraved on the bottom of the base. The pawnbroker knows it must be stolen property from the Los Angeles School District.

These two brothers have been tagging the school for months and are finally caught, thanks to Sofie's identification of the one boy who fingers the real culprits. Taggers all know each other's tagging crew signs, but they rarely tell on one another. This time, however, enough pressure is put on the innocent one so that the guilty ones are identified.

111

Sofie is thankful that day the guilty parties are not one of her own students. She is also thankful that the police who caught the ones who really did the damage. She is thankful the police located the missing microscope, soon to be returned. But she gets no thanks for her part in solving the crime, only a warning from Mr. Griswold saying, "You really should lock up those microscopes."

CHAPTER 28

MATH MANIPULATIVES AND THE M&M WARS

With only a few weeks of school left until Christmas break and the end of Track B, the math department decides to send all math teachers to a math conference. In the past, the math chairman never gave Sofie so much as a "Howdy," let alone help for her two math classes. Now finally, Sofie is included. The conference is out by the airport, two hours from Sofie's house on the busiest Christmas shopping Saturday of the year. If that is not enough to keep teachers away, the torrential rains do that day. Even though principals are invited, and four other teachers signed up, Sofie is the only one to show up from John Quincy Junior High.

The latest big thing in math is "Manipulatives" and "Hands-On." Math experts theorize students cannot conceptualize math principals, without something concrete to count or move around with their hands. Math Manipulatives are supposed to be the savior of our math classes, teaching students what all of us know in our heads. Yes, experts claim math teachers cannot teach effectively without manipulatives, and every school district wants math teachers to replace parts of the math curriculum with the new math manipulative units.

With two weeks to go before the end of the semester, Sofie thinks she can use the math manipulative lesson plans the last week of school. The last week is traditionally a dead week. All the grades are in and text books collected. Yet, Mrs. Castillo still wants the teachers to teach up to the last day, and *no* parties.

During this all-day conference, math teachers from all schools in the district learn how to use multicolored jelly beans to calculate three bean salads using different combinations of the jelly beans. They learn how to calculate ratios and percentages of red, green, yellow, and brown colored M&M candies in a given bag. They learn all that and more. Math manipulatives sounds good and tastes good. It works well for math teachers with the required four-year degree in mathematics, plus one extra year to earn their teaching credentials. Math manipulatives is supposed to be extremely useful teaching English as a Second Language (ESL) students, some of whom do not speak English well...if at all.

Sofie thinks she can try out these new math manipulatives on her eighth-grade and ESL math classes. It can be sort of a treat for her math students, who do not get as many labs as her science students. *They'll love it.* Sofie ponders the fun they will have while learning math. *Nice way to end the semester.* She smiles to herself.

***

Standing in the candy isle of Ralph's supermarket, the first thing Sofie realizes, *this lab is going to cost a lot!* "Let's see," Sofie thinks out loud. "One bag of M&M candies for each group of four," she does the math. *I wonder if the cost of supplies for the candy lab are reimbursable. Probably not.* Sofie opens her purse and pulls out her checkbook. "Let's see how much I had left in my account. Ninety-seven dollars and forty-three cents left. That's enough, I guess, to splurge on supplies. Is that enough to last until the end of the month when my paycheck comes? Oh, what the heck," she says, "I'm going to give it a try."

Going back to her calculations, she mutters "Now, where was I? Oh yes, one bag of M&Ms for each group of four. Two classes with twenty-four students in one class and thirty-six in the other. Let's see, that's sixty students. Sixty divided by four. Okay, I'll need fifteen bags of M&Ms to do the M&M Math Manipulatives Lab. Now at forty-five cents a bag, let's see, that's what, *SEVEN DOLLARS AND TWENTY CENTS* for one day's lab." Words tumble out of Sofie's mouth like hot steaming cocoa burning her tongue. The cost is far more than Sofie expects.

"Oh well," Sofie frowns. "Maybe I can deduct the cost of the candy somehow from my income taxes." Sofie reaches up to the second shelf from the top of the candy section and counts out the fifteen bags of M&Ms and drops them into her shopping cart. Then she adds an extra bag for good luck. If she has good luck teaching the lab, she will eat the extra bag herself. If she miscounted, there goes the extra bag of M&Ms.

Now for the jelly beans, she ponders. "I need seven different colors for the Jelly Bean Math Manipulatives Lab," she says out loud. Carefully she unrolls seven plastic bags at the bulk candy display and tears off each one to fill with jelly beans. Decision time. She must choose seven different colors of jelly beans. The choices are staggering. *"Well, best to stick with the primary colors as much as possible, she thinks. Let's see, Cherry Red, Lemon Drop Yellow, Grannie Apple Green, Blueberry Blue, that's four, what else? Oh, yeah, black and white, of course! Licorice for black and Coconut for white. Now I need one more. Tangerine for orange. Perfect, that will do it."*

Pleased with herself, Sofie lifts the lid of each plastic bin and carefully measures one scoop of each chosen jelly bean flavor into separate bags, wraps the plastic tie around each bag and places the bags into her shopping cart next to the sixteen bags of M&Ms.

Triumphantly, Sofie whirls her shopping cart around and heads for the checkout. Sofie started her shopping for the lab right after school let out. Now it is 5:30 in the evening. She did not think it would take an hour and forty-five minutes, but there she is, in line with everyone else shopping after work.

The long lines stretch out into the aisles. An old lady, two customers ahead of her, nervously fidgets with her black handbag. She is no more than five feet tall, her back is bent over in the shape of a question mark from advanced age. Her short curly silver hair shimmers under florescent lights in the market. She wears baggy, black polyester pants held up with elastic, and a dark blue long sleeve sweater, buttoned up in the front, showing only the white collar of her blouse underneath. When she gets to the cashier, she pulls out a grocery receipt to show the clerk behind the counter.

"You charged me too much on the banana's I bought here yesterday. The bananas are on sale for fifty-nine cents a pound and the cashier charged me sixty-nine cents!" Her high-pitched voice lets everyone in line know her grievance.

"But lady," the cashier explains, "the bananas just went on sale today."

"Well, the bananas are mushy! No good. Not even worth fifty-nine cents. I want my money back." The old lady insists on a refund, wagging her bony finger at the cashier. In the meantime, the checkout line is growing.

"But lady, where are the bananas?" the cashier asks, looking down at the angry old lady.

"I ate them," the old lady says flatly. Then reaching into her big purse, the old woman pulls out a plastic bag with three banana skins and four unpeeled bananas. "Here's proof."

The clerk behind the counter stares down at the open bag of half eaten bananas in disgust and reaches for the loud speaker intercom to call the store manager. "Tom, uh, we have a return over here. Will you please come to aisle four?"

Sofie looks at her watch again. It's already six o'clock. She glances at the other check out lines and they are even longer than hers. By now the store manager, a big man with thick black hair and bushy mustache, arrives. The old lady is telling him the problem with the bananas. The store manager just nods at everything she says. Then he whispers something to the cashier and smiles at the old lady. The cashier gives the old lady what she wants, the difference between the fifty-nine-cent bananas and the sixty-nine-cent bananas, a total of thirty cents.

The line starts to move again, as the old lady shuffles away in triumph. The short baldheaded man behind Sofie says to her, "At last. I didn't think they'd ever get rid of that old lady."

"Yes, I know." Sofie replies politely, doing her best to avoid looking at the way the overhead lights cast reflections on his balding head.

"Well, I guess the old lady got exactly what she wanted, didn't she?

"She certainly did."

Then the baldheaded man looks down into Sofie's shopping cart at all the candy. "Got a sweet tooth, have you?" the man says with a smile, trying to start another conversation with Sofie. Clearly, he is trying to pick her up, but he is not Sofie's type. Not even close.

"Well, no." Sofie says. Ignoring the man behind her, she turns back to face the front of the line and rolls her eyes. Just the smell of his overpowering body odor turns her stomach and she just wants to get out of that market.

The line is moving again, and it is her turn at last. Sofie unloads the bags of M&Ms on the moving conveyor belt and then seven plastic bags of different colored jelly beans.

"Got a sweet tooth?" asks the checkout clerk, as she scans the prices of the candy.

"No. It's not for me. I mean, it's not for me to eat. I'm a teacher. It's for the new math manipulatives lab. We teach math with hands-on labs." Sofie says proudly.

"Wow, when I was in school, we had to learn the hard way, out of the book. Did you get permission slips from the kids' parents and their dentist? Ha ha, just kidding," the clerk jokes.

"Yummy," remarks the baldheaded man behind Sofie. "Can I be in your math class?"

Sofie rolls her eyes again. "Just tell me how much," she says to the clerk.

"Thirty-two, sixty-four," the clerk replies, placing the bags of jelly beans and M&Ms in a plastic grocery bag.

"What!" Sofie cries out. Does she hear the amount, correctly?

"Thirty-two dollars and sixty-four cents," repeats the clerk.

"How much were the jelly beans?" Sofie asks.

"Twenty-five dollars and forty-four cents," the clerk replies, then adds, "There's no tax on food."

"Thanks," Sofie replies, stunned at the cost of her first math lab. Slowly she opens her purse and pulls out her check book. "Wow, that's a third of what I have left in my account." Sofie writes out the check to the supermarket for the thirty-two dollars and sixty-four cents." In her mind, she calculates, *with thirty-two dollars and sixty-four cents, I could've treated myself to a steak dinner with wine and gone to the movies.* But instead, thirty-two dollars and sixty-four cents worth of candy is all for the noble cause of teaching math with manipulatives.

***

What worked for experienced math teachers with years of college math behind them, does not work well for Sofie's eighth grade math students. It does not work at all for her seventh, eighth, and ninth grade ESL math students, the ones who know very little English. In fact, when Sofie's aide, Hector, tells the class in Spanish about the Candy Lab, the ESL students scream with delight.

"I want candy!"

"Gimme Candy!"

"Please teacher, gimme candy!"

Whereas Sofie's eighth-grade math class just ate the jelly beans without first calculating with them. All pandemonium breaks loose in the ESL math class. There are students running around stealing other students' jelly beans. Shouts of unfairness in Spanish and broken English. Jelly beans on the floor and anywhere else you could imagine. *Twenty-five dollars and forty-four cents for one day's lab to end up like this?*

"What a waste of money. Any sane person would have guessed that this is exactly what would happen," Sofie voices her concerns.

"Maybe the M&M Lab will have better results." After all, Sofie rationalizes, "This is a learning experience. Surely, I've learned from my mistakes on the Jelly Bean Manipulatives, haven't I?"

Wrong again. The great M&M wars break out among the groups. Mass stealing, throwing, eating, and playing, all this chaos in both classes is the only result of fifteen bags of M&M candies.

"*Never again,*" Sofie vows, eating the last of the M&M candies from the sixteenth bag. As she sweeps up the floor of her classroom, covered with a scattering of candy wrappers and M&Ms, she promises herself once again, "Math Manipulatives? *Never again.*"

CHAPTER 29

THE LAST DAY'S LESSON: TAGGING ON...

L ooking back at the last day of class, Sofie's heart softens for her junior high students. She knows she will never see those faces again, because she does not plan to renew her teaching contract. Teaching at the junior high school level is just too mentally, physically, and emotionally draining. She does not want to end up like Mrs. Vierma, on Lithium, tranquilized in a mental institution, for burnt out teachers.

Besides, the long, long commute from South Orange County to Los Angeles, has taken its toll on her old car. Strange noises rumble beneath the hood of her ancient red Toyota. Teaching does not pay enough to buy a newer vehicle, and she does not want to end up stranded with a broken car along the side of the freeway at rush hour.

But for the last day, she decides to give her students a lesson they will all enjoy. The principal, Mrs. Castillo, wants teachers to teach to the last day and orders NO parties.

The students all beg for free time.

"Oh, please Ms. Rich, don't make us work on the last day."

"Not the last day, Ms. Rich. Please."

"Let us have free time. Okay, Ms. Rich?"

"Can't we just have free time on our last day, Ms. Rich?" they all plead.

119

Sofie smiles and then says, "No, we will have a lesson." She first reads to her students, the story of the candy cane. Then gives each of her students a candy cane to taste the sweetness of the Christmas season. She thinks, *is this a manipulative, hands-on lesson or what?*

Then, for her first class, Sofie gets butcher paper and colored chalk from the supply room. She covers the two huge chalk boards and the back wall with the butcher paper, so that three fourths of the walls are covered with paper. Then giving each student a piece of colored chalk, tells them they can draw or write anything they want, just if they stay on the paper and write nothing vulgar.

Sofie watches the bliss on their young faces.

Some question, "Can we draw, Ms. Rich? Can we really draw anything?"

"Yes," Sofie answers in a single word.

She smiles. Her eyes twinkle observing how the kids are immediately drawn to the paper. At first, they draw Christmas trees, and snow-covered houses, even though it never snows in Los Angeles. Someone draws a Santa Claus.

Another student writes, *Merry Christmas, Ms. Rich. Happy New Year, from all your friends*, and all the students sign their names.

The next classes come in one period at a time through out the day. Each class, after hearing the story of the candy cane and receiving one, begin drawing and writing with the colored chalk.

But then some students start crossing out names and rewriting their names bigger and bigger. And then other students start drawing hearts and arrows.

Then other students write, *Jose loves Nancy.*

And then *Edith is a Bitch!*

The lesson goes downhill from there.

And so ends Sofie's first and last year of teaching in Los Angeles. As she types her story and collects unemployment, her sanity returns. "Better unemployment compensation than disability insurance like Mrs. Vierma," she says with a wink.

THE END

Sofie Richmond's
Math Manipulatives

Math Manipulatives are used to visualize abstract math concepts.

M&M Labs

Small bags of M&Ms can be used for learning fractions and ratios. Such as:

1. How many red M&Ms are in the whole bag? If there are 5 reds to 25 in the whole bag, then $5 / 25 = 1/5$ of the bag is red M&Ms.
2. How many red M&Ms compared to green M&Ms? If there are 2 greens, then the ratio is 5 reds to 2 greens, or 5 | 2.
3. If you take out all the reds and greens, how many are left? Add the reds and greens then subtract from the whole. All M&Ms − (reds + greens) = others. $25 − (5 + 2) = 18$.

Jelly Bean Labs
Three Bean Salad

Jelly beans can be used like the M&Ms or given a "recipe" the ratio of beans is given to make the "Three Bean Salad." 5 yellow beans to 3 black beans to 4 red beans. How many of each bean is needed to make a salad of 60? Add the three beans and divide the whole: $60 / (5Y + 3B + 4R) = 60 / 12 = 5$.

Shapes

Marshmallows and toothpicks can be used to form shapes as squares, triangles, and other geometric shapes.

Fractions

A paper plate can be used to show many portions such as 2 for halves, 3 for thirds, 4 for fourths, and so on.

Measurements

Kitchen items such as measuring cups and spoons can be used to demonstrate milliliters, ounces, other measurements using beans or rice.

Sofie Richmond's Junior High Laboratory Experiments

Dancing Raisins Experiment:
This experiment is to demonstrate Archimedes' Principle.

Materials Needed: Raisins, Glass of Water, Alka-Seltzer tablets
Preparation: Soak 8 to 10 raisins in water overnight.
Procedure: Fill a clear glass with ordinary tap water. Drop presoaked raisins in the water. Drop one Alka-Seltzer tablet in the water and watch the raisins dance.

How Does It Work?

The raisins will bob up and down for several minutes. Since the surface of the raisins is rough, tiny bubbles of carbon dioxide gas are attracted to it. These bubbles increase the volume of the raisin substantially but contribute very little to its mass. As a result, the overall density of the raisin is lowered, causing it to be carried upward by the denser fluid surrounding it.

Archimedes' Principle states that the buoyant force exerted on a fluid is equal to the weight of fluid displaced. Since the raisins now have a greater volume, they displace more water, causing the fluid to exert a greater buoyant force. The buoyant force of the surrounding fluid is what pushes the raisins to the top.

Once the raisins reach the top, the bubbles pop upon exposure to the air. This makes the raisins denser, causing them to sink. As more bubbles adhere to the raisins, the density of the raisins decreases, and they rise to the surface again. This experiment very clearly shows that an increase in volume will lead to a decrease in density. The bubbles that attach themselves to the raisins are like little life jackets that make the raisins more buoyant by increasing their volume.

Bubble Gum Experiment:
This experiment is to measure the amount of sugar in gum.

Materials Needed: Bubble Gum in single serving in a paper wrapper (like Bazooka), a scale that measures milliliters or ounces.

Procedure: Weigh gum in the wrapper and record the exact weight. Unwrap gum and chew until the gum loses its flavor and sweetness. Weigh the chewed gum on the paper wrapper. Record the exact weight. The chewed gum will weigh less. Now subtract the weight of the chewed gum from the weight of the unchewed gum. The difference will be the amount of sugar in the gum.

About the Author

SYLVIA WEISS SINCLAIR is a first generation American on her father's side; her mother was also born of immigrant parents. She was born in Los Angeles, California and started journaling when she was thirteen years old, continuing throughout her life.

In Glendale High School, Sylvia fell in love with Chemistry. She wanted to be like Madame Curie, working in a laboratory. She went on to Glendale College, majoring in Chemistry.

In 1966, she applied at a laboratory as a lab assistant, but they were not hiring women.

Ten years later, she enrolled in California State University and earned a Bachelor of Arts in Business. She applied to CPA firms, but they were not hiring married women with children. After ten years working as an accountant, Sylvia went back to California State University. She earned a Teaching Credential in Secondary Education, teaching in Los Angeles for only one year.

She now lives in Bay Minette, Alabama with her husband Mike and two cats, Peaches and Mikey. Sylvia is member of the Fairhope Writers' Group, the Alabama Writers' Forum, and the Alabama Writers Conclave. *Fledermama's Son* is her first published novel, based on her travels to Romania.

Coming Soon
THE GHOST OF DYAS CREEK

August 1922 – Deep in the southern Alabama woods, where the long leaf pines stretch to the sky, Margaret steps out of the old wooden farmhouse on a clear, balmy night. Her eyes catch something bright and shadowy moving out of the forest. It takes on the shape of an old man with a long white beard. His hands are reaching out, beckoning Margaret.

CPSIA information can be obtained
at www.ICGtesting.com
Printed in the USA
FFHW02n1108040918